Shadows of Your Black Memory

Shadows of Your Black Memory

Donato Ndongo

Translated and with a Postscript by Michael Ugarte

SWAN ISLE PRESS

CHICAGO

Donato Ndongo was born in Equatorial Guinea. He has published novels, poetry, and essays on postcolonial Africa. His most recent novel is *El metro*. He lives in Spain.

Michael Ugarte is professor emeritus at University of Missouri-Columbia whose works include translations and publications on modern peninsular Spanish and postcolonial literature.

Swan Isle Press, Chicago 60640-8790
©2007, 2016 by Swan Isle Press
All rights reserved. Published 2007
Printed in the United States of America

21 20 19 18 17 16   2 3 4 5
ISBN-13: 978-0-9748881-2-5 (cloth)   ISBN-13 978-0-9972287-0-0 (paperback)

Originally published in Spanish as *Las tinieblas de tu memoria negra*. ©1987 by Donato Ndongo-Bidyogo; ©1987 by Editorial Fundamentos; reprinted ©2000 by Ediciones del Bronce (Grupo Planeta). Published in French as *Les ténèbres de ta mémoire*, ©2004 by Éditions Gallimard.

An earlier version of "Chapter O," translated by Michael Ugarte, appeared in *Raritan Review* 24, no. 1 (summer 2004): 1–11. Reprinted here with permission of the *Raritan Review*.

Jacket illustration and interior page 1: Four-Faced Helmet Mask (Ngontang). Gabon: Fang; early 20th century; wood, kaolin, paint; H/ 34 cm. Collection of the Israel Museum, Jerusalem; gift of Lawrence Gussman, Scarsdale, New York, to American Friends of the Israel Museum, in memory of Dr. Albert Schweitzer. Photograph © The Israel Museum, Jerusalem B97/0006. Spanish Cross, ©iStockphoto.com/George Argyropoulos.

Library of Congress Cataloging-in-Publication Data
    Ndongo-Bidyogo, Donato, 1950-
    [Tinieblas de tu memoria negra. English]
    Shadows of your black memory / Donato Ndongo ; translated and
    with a postscript by Michael Ugarte.
    p. cm.
    Includes bibliographical references.
    ISBN 978-0-9748881-2-5 (hardcover : alk. paper)
    I. Ugarte, Michael, 1949- II. Title.
PQ8619.N363T5613 2007
863'.64--dc22   2007033981

Swan Isle Press gratefully acknowledges that this book has been made possible, in part, with the support of generous grants from:
    The Program for Cultural Cooperation between Spain's Ministry of Culture and United States
        Universities.
    The Illinois Arts Council, a State of Illinois agency

    Europe Bay Giving Trust

www.swanislepress.com

Contents

For my master I write what I saw on the map of the universe: document
of the future that lives in the past, the book of the Exodus-Return.

—Abd al-Wahhab Al-Bayyati
Love Poems Facing the Seven Porticoes to the World

Jealously kept by the loyal shadows of your black memory.

—L. S. Senghor
Chants d'ombre

Shadows of Your Black Memory

zero

His mouth exhaled a unique odor, a mixture of garlic, parsley, and pipe tobacco. It was a strong smell, sweet and pungent. His thick lips moved slowly as if he were tired of speaking. His eyes, once blue, a mere hint of their former brilliance, were fixed impertinently on my face. Yes, with loving impertinence.

He was fighting baldness. It was a desperate battle; defeat was a certainty. I stared at his hairline curving inward at the temples where a few hairs remained erect, determined not to abandon the wrinkled leather of his brow. The jugular vein in his stiff white neck cast a red shadow on his face. His Adam's apple stood out like a mountain in the shimmering light of a late afternoon. His wrinkled hands and fingers drummed on the table to the beat of his words. I observed his gentle demeanor, the short, deliberate cadences of his speech, a pace that almost bored me as I listened. The tediousness was too much for me as I scrutinized that lean, austere face, that small nose, those tartar-filled teeth yellowing in deference to the authority of his pipe. Or I simply observed the somber adornments of the room, sparsely furnished, uninviting, gray smoke filling the air and shattering my illusions.

As always, he had summoned me to his office unexpectedly.

"Yes," he told me, "there are things only you can experience, terribly alone. You complain? You should know that this is one of the conditions of your ambition, the control of your life that you so desire. Pride in that separation from others? Why? I see much sadness in it, too much to search for real satisfaction or pride. Your doubts cause your friends to shun you; true, this is deadly. They shrug their shoulders at you, some because they are exaggerating what they think you demand of them, others because you seem to disdain them. You seem to lock yourself up inside. Others, well...The complaints are infinite, and they produce a kind of alienation that you accept without bitterness, without hatred or rancor, but it makes you doubt, it makes you suffer."

And I thought about Juan Luis, who had been my confidant, the first one I spoke with in earnest; he was about to abandon me. And about José Vicente, who several times treated me in public as if I were a crackpot or a starry-eyed idealist. And even Carlos, who was always telling me about projects I knew he would never finish. And about Julián, who had been so influenced by José Vicente; the two of them, under the slightest provocation, made sure they found fault with my new views. And Esteban, the one I had traveled with on the ship from Guinea, intending or hoping that we would become priests—who knows under what spell?—Esteban was the one who treated me like an upstart in front of everybody. But above all I thought about Angeles and her last letters, her serenity, a picture of peace: How many things change in such a short time, Angeles! Here I am in front of him, remembering you, your white figure, so alluring, and wanting to rush out to write you tirelessly, as my one and only diversion. Perhaps if I don't write those letters to you, I'll write them for myself, for my own satisfaction, for my own justification, as if it were a way out of this. I don't know. I can no longer do anything about it; I don't know, forgive me, it's like a pleasant addiction, a slow passion, and you at a distance...

"You may choose," the old rector continued. "You can be bold enough to take this rough path alone, or you can go along with everybody else, following them, keeping in step. If you choose the first path, you'll be a first-rate explorer. But choosing the second will merely keep you in line; you'll do mediocre work, unworthy of your talent."

He looked at me sympathetically, perceiving my consternation, totally aware of my sadness, and he added,

"But why talk of loneliness, my son? A Christian is never alone."

For the first time I felt an impulse of affection and goodwill toward him.

"And all this, Reverend Father," I pleaded, "isn't it...?"

"What?" he asked anxiously. "What, my friend?"

"Well...pride, a kind of presumption...?"

I waited for his response, my heart beating, knowing I was about to make a life choice or, more precisely, to choose a path, construct my life, adorn it, elevate it.

"Pride?" he objected in a low voice. "Pride?...My friend, pride is when we're convinced of our own excellence and forget the perfection of God."

And then he said, surely knowing how I would respond:

"Is that you?"

"No, Reverend Father," I answered too quickly, as if to cover my doubts. "I don't think that for a moment."

"My son," he replied, "your soul is weak, unwilling to see anything but weakness. Why do you doubt the high path God has called you to? My son, you will find God not only at the end of an arduous ascent, but at each step, at each moment. And humility consists precisely in recognizing that we have no power against this everlasting presence."

Angeles once again penetrated my thoughts; I remembered my last time with her. It was a Sunday on one of those brief, gloomy weekends; we had decided to take advantage of the short time we had together. We went to the banks of the dry riverbed on the deserted outskirts of the city, modernist buildings on one side and boundless countryside on the other. Walking along the riverbed, we encountered a gypsy family making their home under a bridge. We spoke with them for a long time, and we forgot we were hungry—the place was saturated with the smell of soft earth, "like the villages in Guinea," I told her. I spoke to her of an ideal land where the mornings were long and the afternoons short, the sun coming down in soft splinters, a gentle breeze, the porous abundance of sand, the rebellious gentleness of dusk, a snail lost in white foam, reflections at high tide, images, memories in which words were like pebbles on a beach with the waves washing over them, and an inexplicable calm. But soon I grew depressed, disgusted, anxious to get out of there. "Maybe you're just a romantic, you love ruins," she said laughing, recalling something someone had said in a dark movie theater when we first went out after knowing each other for so long, loving each other at a distance with the roar of your longed-for words, the purity of distance. And I felt that nothing tied me there, I didn't expect anything anymore, I didn't know what would become of me, what it was all for, what was the use of living that way, the routine, no incentive, as if I were in the corner of a planet stopped in its orbit, compliant, accepting the same old patterns so far from my real self that they didn't make me feel better, obeying and respecting interests I no longer cared about in the least.

"My son, I'm not trying to convince you of anything," said the rector. He seemed to have discovered that there was no hope for me, that I was escaping forever. "But I imagine you've thought it through. Am I mistaken?"

"No, Reverend Father. You're not mistaken at all."

The words had come out quickly, in sharp contrast to the old priest's measured speech. The first winds of a tempest gathering in your tormented soul, the signs are there, I'm ready, I can't go back now, I must go forward. I wonder what my father would think about this? To abandon it would be to abandon my parents, but I must break loose, now, so many years waiting to say it, and now I can't get beyond circumlocutions, and what will happen to me when the wall holding up the bridge crumbles? Now or never, I'm ready to face everything, let the chalice of my earthly salvation come to me, let it recover who I am, individually and collectively. I must not go through this life without leaving something behind, but he won't believe it, he'll think it's about something else. And this doesn't even have anything to do with you, Angeles. But it doesn't matter: it's important to seize every opportunity, the slightest opportunity, to tell him, to explain, to reveal my decision, *ir-re-vers-i-ble*, to go another way. There's a battle hovering above the tribe, a great conflict that some time ago had drawn a great ring around the moon. A large hot moon, icon of your ancestral strength, guiding you through dark nights, there, then, here, always, a trusty lantern that makes a fearless man out of you. Let there be light, and there was light: the clarity of the moon has illuminated my spirit, the decision has won over my doubts, the clear path winds through the thick green forest, an immense expanse, curves without danger, a tenuous slope I can take cautiously and passionately like a patient, watchful hunter.

Perhaps to nudge the moment along, a moment that seemed to stand still, the imploring voice of the old rector broke in.

"Is all this enough?" And he kept penetrating my soul with his gaze. As he chose his words, his whole body accentuated what he said.

"I think it's enough, father."

He remained pensive, although he didn't appear to be thinking. The fingers on his left hand kept drumming on an open book; the index finger of his right hand holding his pipe; all of him made me sad. Finally he spoke.

"Son, being a priest is the most arduous path a man can take, especially in these days of materialism and modernism. I'm sure you've noticed it. Not everyone is capable of putting up with a life like this, a life dedicated to God and to others..."

He cut off his own words, once again lost in self-absorption. He wasn't smoking. And the seconds passed by slowly. And the wind howled furiously against the coarse wooden shutters. The spring sun slid out of sight, the afternoon had grown cool.

"...only the faithful souls, only the truly strong can hold up until the end. And I think you are one of them, despite your apparent lack of defenses."

With the first puff from his pipe I felt his expansive gaze on my face. And I had turned my eyes to the ivory crucifix on the front of his desk.

"I had hoped you would stay on. Summer is a good time to temper emotions and regain strength. I have faith in you. Men like you are the ones who can inculcate the essential doctrine of Christ among your people. We outsiders have already accomplished our mission; times have changed and we must understand and cope. The African church doesn't have enough priests among its own people, ones who speak the local language.

"We've sown the seeds that must bear fruit among you. Our time is up, we brought the voice of Christ to your land; we carried out our mission in difficult times, bravely, always with the contentment of winning over new souls for the Supreme Master's flock. You are our pride and justification. Your job is to remain committed, to look deeper, correct the errors, become apostles among your people, balance the scales in the ups and downs awaiting you."

"Africa doesn't only need priests, father. In my country," I continued timidly and humbly, "there are barely any doctors, engineers, lawyers, and so forth...among the natives. These are crucial too, father, to achieve stability, progress, to construct a nation. I've come to realize this and..."

He cut me off with a just a hint of anger.

"You are right, my son; no doubt all that is necessary. But everyone has his station in life. Economists and lawyers will always be around. But if the Lord has called upon you as an apostle, there is no reason to be anything else..."

And I noticed how the lines on his forehead disappeared, and I admired the supreme effort he was making to control himself. He remained silent for a few moments, regained composure, and added:

"My words come from the profound bitterness your desertion would cause. Yes, my friend, it would be a desertion, like fleeing the battlefield. I suffer your anguish with you, your anxiety, your...how should I put it, your inner conflict. You have almost reached the end of the process, and you will come out victorious. I have faith in you as an apostle among your own."

"And I will be an apostle, father, you can count on it. Only I'll be among them, in their time. I need you to understand me. I don't aspire to be anything but a man among others, to find peace, without mystifications. Neither half a man nor a superman. I don't want veneration or dishonor; I don't need to feel guilty about anything, and I don't want anyone to laugh at me. The kind of priest that abounds in Africa makes me very nervous, the inspired ones, cheating and lazy." I paused to take in his reaction. "But this isn't the real reason for my leaving, father. I don't feel as though I've been called by God to this mission. It weighs on me that I received my minor orders knowing that I didn't deserve them, and I can't go on. I had this feeling some time ago, but I doubted, I fought with myself, I asked for guidance. And because my soul can no longer endure such a conflict, it's time to put an end to it: I don't have the vocation to be a priest, father."

True, it wasn't difficult for me to say this; the fear was no longer in me, and it was as if ancestral power were speaking for me. The moon had become radiant, but I felt no relief. The weary victory you feel after a successful battle, a satisfied soul, stretched muscles, all kept me from embarking on a march to the future, in spite of the brilliant moon illuminating my life path and revealing what was essential, free of fantasy. The old priest had turned his eyes to the ivory crucifix, and as he emptied his pipe into an ashtray with a fake Arab motif—the only object that made his huge office look human—an aura of melancholy came over his thin face and neck reddened by the suddenly swollen jugular vein. In the distance, the chapel bells began to chime for dinner. He arose from his chair, and so did I.

❋

It's autumn. It's raining. It's cold, but you don't notice it. It's wretched weather, making you uncomfortable and bringing back memories of a childhood that forever conditions your existence. Through the shutters, half open to take advantage of the final rays of sun, you hear the echo of the restless coming and going of the city dwellers. The exasperating yet sublime monotony of raindrops against the windowpane evokes a vastly different scene—jubilant nature against trees of cement and glass—a scene you captured from your window when you were in the seminary in Banapa.

Yes, this is an afternoon to remember.

one

The image of my father: a tall, thin black man, a firm disposition; at a particular point in his life he decided to collaborate with the white colonizer. He built himself a large concrete house with a shiny zinc roof that stood out among the grass-roofed mud buildings surrounded by wilderness. He was the first to dig a privy ditch in the patio, hidden by a hut of whose function few were aware: it was to keep us from defecating under the coffee groves so that the chickens wouldn't peck at the excrement. He was among the first in the area, if not the very first, to plant coffee, the sign of new times and modernity. My father thought about all of us, his eight children by just one wife—I was the firstborn. He wanted us to be the extensions of his illusions. It was clear to all, although no one said so, that my father had abandoned the traditions of his people for the sake of civilization. This is why my father is a black man who does everything on a grand scale, like the whites, and this is why he commands respect, perhaps even fear, and it's why the missionaries and the police in charge of our district stay at our house when they visit the village. It's a village like many others in the area, with lines of grass and adobe houses, a few made of wood, built willy-nilly as if they wouldn't be there tomorrow, on both sides of the dusty road. A church stood out in the midst of the other buildings, a crude wooden cross on top, and next to it was the school, also constructed with local materials; every now and then it had to be spruced up like the others.

Father Ortiz arrived on his motorcycle. After he picked me up, we spent two or three days inspecting the alterations to the small chapels that had been erected in clearings in the jungle; we rode on impassible trails, sometimes in the rain with branches whacking at my face, and I protected myself from them and from the wind as I pressed against the priest's sweaty back, and that's how I discovered that white people smell different—like white people, I guess. I saw the nape of his neck covered with mosquito bites—a sight I'll never forget: he had the skin of a plucked chicken, a pith helmet bouncing on his small head and tied under his perfectly shaved chin, and sweat stains getting bigger and bigger until they covered his entire back, his skin showing through his white satin cassock like a crystal tongue. I often had to grab onto his black sash so that I wouldn't fall off his motorcycle, my nose pressing against his hard spine, and instead of feeling pain I smelled his aftershave in the wind. And the flaps of his black sash were like magnets attracting burrs, the same as his pant legs, his cassock tucked under his belt, and his black nylon socks; I helped him rearrange his vestments at the outskirts of the village so that he'd look presentable. But mud was embedded under our fingernails; we almost always arrived terribly dirty, though it was less noticeable in the priest's case because he could cover himself with his cassock before entering a village so that his soiled pants didn't show. The worst thing about the jungle is not the insects, nor even the wild animals. The bush is beautiful: the cool, refreshing shade, the birdsong, the yelping of monkeys, the abundance of ripe fruit mixed with the fragrance of coffee groves, brilliant patches of sky barely perceptible between shiny moist leaves, the tenuous murmur of the breeze moving through the trees, the fleeting image of an animal startled by the noise of the motorcycle. But it would have been a lot more beautiful if I had only worn long pants. The worst thing about the jungle is the grass scraping your skin. I arrived with my legs and thighs burning; I had spent all night scratching intensely (pleasure and pain) despite the neighbors' waiting for us with washbowls of warm water. As Father Ortiz's altar boy, I was afforded early privileges, like eating dinner with him: chicken with tomatoes and olive oil, canned sardines, cookies, and sometimes even bread. Yes, the priest was a very important man, someone sent by God once a month to bring us the Holy Word. In the villages there was nothing that made life on earth more agreeable, the anticipation of heaven waiting for us all—who knows, waiting for me too as the Lord's apostle who has devoted his life to the conversion of heathens. I learned to recite the Mass in Latin, to order all the ornaments for the different liturgical functions, to eat with a knife and fork and chew with my mouth shut. I learned much from Father Ortiz, but above all to be like the whites, educated, well mannered, and distant.

At that time I was going to school in the village. Don Ramón was a good teacher—at least, I remember him fondly: his remarkable height, his no less remarkable slimness, his starched, clean-smelling elegance, despite his always walking around with a *melongo* whip, for he upheld the maxim "Spare the rod and spoil the child"—he repeated it to us all the time, even more so when it came to black children because of our very thick heads. Not knowing your lesson could cost you twenty-five or thirty lashes on your bare butt, and to tell the truth, Don Ramón's students went home from school knowing everything he taught us, since it was always better to study a little than to finish the morning with a bloody rear end or your knees lacerated from being forced to kneel in the gravel. Those were times of hope, a somber hope as I remember it; sometimes you could hear just one yell above the whirr of the thrashing, and a hope was destroyed. But I never had occasion to experience Don Ramón's expediting pedagogy on my body.

At eight o'clock each morning we had to gather at the school with one arm raised in a patriotic fascist salute, and then strut military style past the red and yellow Spanish flag that he had raised with infinite respect and solemnity, as we fervently sang, *I come to school eager to learn, Lord, let me be a humble prodigy, let me please you, O God of my life.* We repeated the lyrics at different pitches until we got to "Lord" in a polyphony dominated by a baritone. We marched fast, while our elders left for their chores in the bush, carrying with them the remembrance of our clear and distant gaze and our uplifted faces: *I go forward with my Mother Spain and onward to God; I wish to honor my Nation; an immense desire urges me forward, lyrically inspiring the duties of my hono-o-o-or.* And that last syllable extended infinitely until it harmonized in rhythm and majesty with a culminating verse that jolted the morning's sleepiness right out of us, tropical grasslands, flags waving, and a soul at peace allowing our will to triumph. We ended promising who knows what to heaven, and even the stars lit up our faith in the imperial path to God through the tropical jungles—there were no snow-capped mountains around there. These were victorious mornings; we were dutifully good-humored even when it rained, facing the sun with our "new black shirts," as in the fascist hymn, all those shiny little black heads, hair cropped short, flies and head lice attracted by the brilliantine ("head lice will be plucked from you with a shaving knife, you pigs!" barked Don Ramón), our white uniforms. We were filled with fervent desire, we were all exuberant, eager to learn why we were fascists and what it was to be a Falangist until victory or death and why we were so glad to be at the service of Spain. And we entered the classroom victoriously, a dusty earth floor below, a grass roof still green; but no one ever explained to us—and we knew no one would ever ask—why our mission was to convince our mothers that when they discovered we were in the Fascist Youth Party, they should embrace us and say, my son, this is what I wanted to see: brave Falangists with a great legacy, raising up Spain Great and Free, and up with the squadrons in victorious battle, indeed there is a new morning in Spain.

In reality, it wasn't memories that came to mind on this lazy afternoon; it was the dark flame of the earth. Don Ramón was dead serious when he cried out patriotically, Long live Franco, up with Spain, viva! Fall out. Franco! and we would hurry into school. It was a huge classroom, crudely divided into the shape of a cross by split tree trunks serving as desks, the real desks hadn't arrived.

In the front-right rows were the highest grades, in the front-left the middle grades, in the back-right the low grades, and in the back-left the preschoolers mixed with a few older ones who couldn't read. And that's how Don Ramón divided the morning classes, teaching the little ones the beginning letters and the alphabet from the *Raya First Grade Book*, then arithmetic and reading to the middle grades, and some basic geography and history from the *Dalmau Carles Pla Encyclopedia* to the elementary grades. But since we were all in the same classroom, we learned a bit of everything. As the children in the first grades got their lessons, the rest of us chattered, and Esimi was incapable of keeping us quiet, no matter how old or strong he was. It all got out of control like an unsettled wasp's nest that not even Don Ramón's rod could suppress. Yes, the more you learned, the closer you got to the podium; it was called Don Ramón's platform. And in a short time you managed to get as far as the first row to the right, whose great advantages you quickly discovered: this was the place of honor set aside for the most studious and best-mannered pupils; from there you could see Don Ramón's handwriting perfectly (clean, careful, neat), his black hands white with chalk. Even more important, however, on the first-row bench to the right you felt closer to the Truth: just by looking over Don Ramón's well-groomed head, your eyes met the direct gaze of the Youngest of Generals in Europe, the Invincible Leader of Spain by the Grace of God, by whose blessing all of you were allowed to break ranks just before and after going into the classroom. Yes. The General was looking directly into my eyes; I will never forget that gaze, severe yet filled with goodness; it left me no choice but obedience and studiousness as was expected of those of us on the first bench, being grateful to that Man who had brought us the True Liberty that the Godless who wanted to destroy us, enslaving us with deceptions and material temptations, those Godless creatures who made up a race all their own, evil people painted in red, whose language sounded like gobbledygook filled with "isms." But the only redeeming "ism" is Catholicism, which preaches the One True Religion and Equality among men facing the Lord on Judgment Day; and when I felt I had enough courage to look away from the Redeeming Chief of State's severe face for a few brief seconds, I looked over to the Martyr Victim of Calumny, the Great Young Hope, Slain by the Villainous Bullets of the Enemies of the Fatherland *forever*, as Don Ramón always used to say when he worked himself into a frenzy telling us the story. But the Founder didn't look straight at me. He looked sad, with an expression of touching melancholy, his face slightly pointed in one direction so as to let us admire him, and I did admire the beauty of his head, balding with perfect symmetry, the broad-lapelled shirt he was wearing allowing us a glimpse of a chest expanding with Generosity. And between each of these portraits hung an enormous bronze crucifix, highlighting the muscular strength of the arms of the Redeemer, his head resting on his chest, his knees arched, a deep wound in his heart, blood dripping from the shiny bronze cavity. Don Ramón said it was blood and water; he showed us with his finger as he grimaced with supreme pain, and despite all the effort of my imagination I could never quite grasp it as drops of blood and water. And his fallen abdomen, yielding to the strength of his body from the waist up, as if his ordeal had made him smaller from the waist down. And I discovered that from behind—as a little boy, I was always imagining and trying to get closer to his eyes—the Christ figure was hollow; he was not a real man, because he didn't have a back, or thighs, or muscles on the backs of his legs, and it made me think twice for many months about his being a real man as well as God, until these thoughts turned into guilt for such early sins against our faith. And I ended up believing that indeed he was a real man as well as God, and maybe it was the Jews who had stripped his entire backside away by leaving him empty during his agony. And in large Gothic letters, on a part of the metal jagged at the edges, as if it had been struck in anger, those insistent letters whose meaning I wanted to know more than anything else in this world and which only fear and the whip prevented me from asking: "INRI."

There were certain moments when a member of the triumvirate who headed our school—a spiritual tripod on which our subsequent awakening would rest—was no longer a personality unto himself, no longer an integral being in our eyes. On Thursdays we said the rosary in school with Don Ramón kneeling on the podium like a silhouette, aware of everything we said, even our gestures. When he sermonized the mysteries of pain, the crucified figure acquired an almost physical suffering. Thursday was the day of Purity, the day consecrated to the Virgin Mary, Saint of all Saints, and this was the day we learned the catechism. But I can no longer remember it with the same precision as on the days Don Ramón spoke about Patriotic Education, always in the final hours of the morning. And I would leave school deeply disturbed by the vile murders of such great figures, still present, but who seemed never to have actually existed. I left filled with indignation about the hordes of men with red skins who burned churches and convents with nuns inside; it was something that none of us heathens had done, they were the true savages. I left school regally indignant at the martyrdom of those gloriously fallen at the hands of the Antichrist, and I didn't know exactly what the Antichrist was because Don Ramón didn't say, but it must have been something terrible like Luzbel. And the pain and desire for patriotic revenge turned into feelings of manliness, the very same manliness that made the Real Spain rise up, answering the call of the Victorious Chief—I looked furtively at the chest of the Most General of Generals, and there was the seal of his mysterious power, an insignia in the shape of a V and T superimposed with a small circle in the middle. And we always ended by singing some patriotic song about King Ferdinand and Queen Isabella and the imperial spirit: "We will die kissing the sacred flag of our glorious Spain, still the powerful nation whose triumphs remain endless." After school I would find myself—when building toy bamboo cars with my cousin Mbo, on any day, anywhere, in my granddad's house or in the bush with Tío Abeso, my uncle Abeso—humming a tune about having a comrade, and that comrade always had the face of the Founder, an image that awakened all my feelings of gratitude and all the fervor of my brief seven years.

Everyone thought you were a smart child, and only you knew you were not. You had the advantage of coming from a family that spoke Spanish correctly, which is why you never had to kneel down on the mound of gravel that Don Ramón kept for the ones who spoke Fang in school in his presence, or even if he merely heard they had done so. Your father's continuous contact with the colonizers, your being an altar boy, and above all the *Little Prayer Book* that Father Ortiz had given you, all this helped you remember and ponder your childhood and the years that eventually brought you here. At an early age you spoke Castilian without mistakes and could read well. Now that everything is passing through your memory as in a movie shown over and over again for years, acknowledge that you wouldn't have been anything if it weren't for that little gift—it was providential. Now that arrogance is subsiding and you see yourself as you are and as you should be and not as they told you to be, accept the fact that you would never have arrived here if it weren't for the *Little Prayer Book*, that little spirituality book, a manual for being a good Christian. And you enthusiastically acquiesced to the recommendations: you recited the three Hail Marys entering or leaving your house, walking past the chapel, before and after meals; and when you heard an ugly word, you covered your ears and made the sign of the cross, trying to repair the damage for the sake of the Lord. I, O God, wish to please you, praise be to God. You even sang a prayer in the ecstasy of devotion; blasphemy is a sin invented by Lucifer; beware, then, of falling into the pit into which he has fallen wretchedly. When you got out of bed, there were morning prayers, matins, followed by lauds, the prime, the rosary, vespers, post-vespers, the angelus at noon; and that's the way it was every day.

You liked the lessons on the history of Spain (they were called "notions"), and when Don Ramón asked you what you were, your little voice stood out clearly: all of us together are Spaniards by the grace of God! And why are we Spanish? intoned Don Ramón, and your clear voice again stood out: we are Spaniards blessed for having been born in a country called Spain. And with Don Ramón's facile explanations you accepted the inexorable and inextricable absurdity of successive centuries: Spaniards had come to save you from anarchy because your ancestors were heathens, barbarians, cannibals, idolaters, who kept cadavers in their dwellings, vestiges of savagery that you censored along with Father Ortiz. Yes, you assisted him, and in all the villages you instructed the black savages to rid themselves of totemic symbols, lances, arrows dipped in poison, masks, wood figurines, bronze effigies, and drums while you spoke of the wrath of God against those who kept the devil inside, and Father Ortiz took all those things away to burn them, or so he said. Like a little Saint Paul wounded by the voice of God, with a convert's enthusiasm or, who knows, the vehemence of a repentant sinner, you feverishly battled the paganism of your people. And you were horrified at seeing how many people of your tribe would not allow the objects of their identity to be expropriated; the elders persisted in refusing to be baptized, knowing that they would never obtain divine grace, which was up to the occupiers, who withheld it unless proof of baptism was shown.

Tío Abeso was a polygamist; he had never entered the grass-roofed chapel and didn't trust whites. He was always quarreling with your father, and when you secretly sided with your father, you still didn't understand that the two represented antagonistic and irreconcilable ways of life in your village at that time. Your uncle was the resister, the one who refused to capitulate, the one who wanted to keep the torch burning; he was the light that your generation was dimming, little by little. And your uncle told you that he had fought against the Spanish troops who arrived ages ago, who knew when, maybe an eternity, and you heard furtive rumors about the embarrassing dismissal of the chief, who had been chosen by consensus, and the rumors were confirmed: he had opposed civilization. But you saw that Tío Abeso still held on to his halo of dignity, perhaps the rumors about him came from his contempt of the white man: how could a man who had six wives and who refused to plant coffee because he thought blacks had no need for it, a man who disdained the advances of civilization, a man who was not even baptized, how could a man like that be placed on the flowered pedestal of the Chief of the Clan? The notions of history that Don Ramón not so much explained as hammered into us and that later you reviewed in the *Dalmau Carles Pla Encyclopedia* by the kerosene light showed clearly that the Spanish had come to liberate you from your bad habits of walking around naked, showing your privates everywhere, eating human flesh, and all that. Because it's only natural that God should send a superior chosen race to save the heathens from eternal damnation, as he had sent Moses to tear away the Israelites from the satanic pharaoh, and just as he had sent those very same Spaniards to other lands filled with unbelievers to Christianize them and bring them Civilization and the One True Doctrine. And the image drawn in the book spoke for itself: Christopher Columbus with his knee to the ground and his sword under his cape, his right hand raised toward heaven; the other conquistadors nestling behind a parapet that shielded them from savage onslaughts; and the naked Indians receiving the message of Revelation for the first time. Don't deny it now. You had already accepted the idea, it had made its way into your soul, that Spanish genius had always distinguished itself in the battle against unbelievers. It had expelled the Christ-killers from its land. The invincible sword of Ferdinand and Isabella, no matter which, both monarchs, both Catholic, had put an end to the idolaters of Allah and his false prophet, restoring the traditional order, and the grace of God rewarded them with the greatest empire the world had ever known on which the sun never set. How can they live in that heat every day, all day long, without sleeping or anything? Don't be stupid and don't bother your brother with your silliness, and Don Ramón's whip moved menacingly. It's that the Spanish race is special, just look at the Counter-Reformation and the just wars against the heretics and the apostates of Flanders and Germany, and look at the Golden Age crowning the whole thing, and Cervantes, the author of the greatest novel in the world; the order established by the infinite wisdom of God could never be altered.And your innocent reasoning power early in your life accepted the whole story of Revelation and all its consequences, as Ambrosio the catechist always said, translating the *Christian's Spiritual Guide*, which he read and commented on every Sunday and on holidays when Father Ortiz was not there; and when he was, Ambrosio would translate his fiery sermons. The catechist looked as though he had actually lived through that fateful day on Gethsemane, so moving were his words.

You were an earnest Christian, yes, a sincere patriot, yes, predestined to be one of them. Like your godfather whom you barely knew but whose life they told you about every night after rosary, before supper, a saintly life that had ended with a real miracle. Every one confirmed they had seen the Blessed Virgin with their own eyes sanctifying the soul of your godfather, a soul ever so white, covered with a chasuble with pure white lace, free of original sin as she received his soul with his very last breath, an ever so beautiful white woman shrouded in a white habit like the ones worn by the nuns where your sister went to school. And in your vivid imagination you saw the transfiguration of the big black body, wide nose, and thick lips—your father saved his photos, now worn and yellowing, the edges torn. Some day, he said, they'll ask me for them to make prints of your godfather when he uttered his last words, *O sweet Mary, be my salvation. Heart of Christ, in you I trust,* and you yearned to live a humble life like your celebrated spiritual hero, your godfather, a life sanctified every moment of its existence by the devotion of the blessed heart of Mary. You wanted to be a worthy godson so that he would not be ashamed of you, so that he would protect you and guide you from his seat of honor on the right hand of Our Lady.

And at night before bed, I had a waking dream, and I saw myself surrounded by angels and archangels, cherubim and seraphim, angelic powers, thrones, and little dominions of chubby cheeks and the blond hair of children waving under the omnipresent and reassuring protection of the Guardian Angel Saint Michael, in whose protecting arms I had just fallen asleep with ejaculatories that were worth at least three hundred indulgences for my sins. Yes, I was a fervent and sincere Catholic, and with pure ardor, sincerity, and humility I had already traced the future of my life, a life having no other purpose than devotion to God, that benevolent and merciful God, the eye of God in a triangle that I had scratched on the headboard of my bed like those figures in my textbook; God sees you, a God who had promised good fortune to the humble at heart, to the poor in spirit, to the hungry and thirsty (justice: all this you would describe many years later). And I did penance, and I tried to avoid eating meat on Fridays, and I said the novena for the Immaculate Conception and then the prayers before Saint Joseph's Day, trying to keep the promise of the first nine Fridays, losing count of the first Saturdays. And above all, you stayed away from bad company, from all the children of your town, from all the brothers of your tribe, because they had not been called by the Holy Spirit, nor were they touched by the grace of God. And every day after the usual rosary before supper I was already tired and would start to nod off. But I was jolted by my father's thumping my cropped head still shiny from the brilliantine. I went on whispering prayers, blessed art though Mary full of grace, and when I finished the rosary I was very tired and went to bed without supper, but I found the strength to kneel down beside my bed, my hands folded and the crown of my head bowed toward my chest, so that I could feel the pure presence of my blessed godfather at my back, the one who was holding the saint's halo in his hands, the very halo that a minute later, fast asleep, I would place on my head.

two

It was when I was six years old, I think, on a Saturday afternoon—
no one told me anything because those things are always better kept
silent—I noticed a strange atmosphere around me; my mother was
roaming around the house dejectedly, upset about who knows what.
She kept eying me stealthily, as if she wanted to protect me from
some impending danger. My father was being kind to me, curiously
kind, and he let me have all the fish and *contriti* that my grandmother, Mama Fina, prepared just for me. It wasn't even my birthday or
my saint's day, and I hadn't done anything special on the previous
few days, except maybe winning a fight with my cousin Mbo, who
was older than I was. But intuition told me that my elders' attitude
was abnormal, even if it was all related to my victory over cousin
Mbo. When my father asked me why I had come home with my body
and clothes all dirty, I dared not tell him the truth: that cousin Mbo

had called me a sissy, so I had to punch him on his big nose, making it bleed; and I told my mother that I had fallen on the road. My father looked at me, all serious, with that stern look that only he can give me, and he shook his finger in front of my eyes, warning me: I don't like lies, son, no one gets their knees and elbows and entire body so beaten up with a little fall. But I couldn't tell him that when I swung at cousin Mbo, the other kids jeered that I wasn't worthy of fighting a man, I was just like a girl, and men don't fight women; get out of here, you're useless and you haven't shed blood for your mother country, the only thing you're good for is eating and shitting and hiding behind women; and then I felt not only shame but anger, and for the first time I was clever about it—now you'll see if I'm a man, don't run away, you cowards—and I was able to show them that I was a man, a brave man capable of catching them and cousin Mbo and of giving him a good swat on his big nose. And that night, while my mother was giving me a bath, I asked her why the other kids called me a girl when it was clear that I peed like a man.

That Saturday afternoon my mother gave me another bath. The twigs and boiled bark were still at the bottom of the basin; the water was reddish and thick, and when it dripped down my face to my lips and into my mouth, I tasted the bitter-sweetness. And my body began to smell sour, a penetrating smell, and my fingers stuck to my body, and instead of drying me with a towel they left me out in the afternoon sunlight, and as the water evaporated, the thick odor got stronger and made me feel bad about myself. And instead of short pants, they dressed me in my *clot*e. And for supper I didn't have tapioca or yams or that delicious palm oil soup my mother made. And even though I wasn't sick, my mother brought me a cup of rare tea that at first tasted sweet, then bitter, and left an aftertaste that made my mouth feel clammy and sour; my tongue felt heavy but my body was weightless, free of all worries or impurity.

I didn't go to church the next day to hear Ambrosio the catechist, and a feeling difficult to define of both excitement and fear came over me for staying alone in bed, because there must have been a reason unknown to me for the way the elders were behaving toward me. Then I saw Tía Te's little head with her pretty braids. And I could see she was in a bad mood. I went up to her to try to make her feel better and suggested we go over to the shed to see if my father had forgotten to close the door, so that we might be able to find the rake and use the long handle to shake the papaya branches, making the ripe fruit fall to the ground. She shook her head, and I wondered whether she didn't like papayas any more, or maybe she no longer liked to play with me, but her eyes were filled with tears, and she told me, crying, that she couldn't eat papaya or anything else. I was used to Tía Te's tears; she was a sensitive fragile little girl. I kept running around the patio pretending I didn't care until she came over to me. She untied the string to the *clote* that was around my neck, and she looked down at the area between my thighs. Why do you have to be a man? she blurted out, and I didn't know what to say because all of a sudden a great doubt came over me whether being a man was a good thing. Her tone was bitter and scornful, but soon I got over it; in the long run I was happy to be a man, I don't know why, maybe because

I hadn't yet learned that men too cry for everything and for nothing. While I retied the string under my chin, I thought seriously about what she had said, and the only thing I could tell her was that I wasn't a man yet, that I was only a boy, although I proudly showed her the wounds on my knees and elbows, implacable symbols of my manly victory over cousin Mbo. You are a man, she said, looking at me no longer disdainfully but with pride or admiration or love, as she always looked at me. And when I objected that no one is a man until mother earth swallows his blood—you see, you have to cut this little piece hanging from here, I said showing it to her—she told me that now she considered me a man because that very afternoon they were going to cut it and mother earth would swallow my blood. I wondered about it, and then I understood a few things, but all of a sudden my mind was clouded and I couldn't keep on thinking. I tried to stay happy, but I didn't know how to laugh; I tried to play, but nothing came out the way I wanted. And I stood there stupefied, thinking that in just a few hours I would no longer be a child, and those cowardly pigs would no longer call me names, shamelessly sucking on their stinky fingers and rubbing them on my chin or calling me a little girl or not letting me play with them or tugging on the front of my thing when they saw I wanted to pee, and running away when I tried to get back at them with a good punch with the excuse that they didn't want to fight a little boy. Just a few hours later, I knew it, I would be just as tall as cousin Mbo and as strong as my dad, and I'd be able to go hunting with Tío Abeso; I'd kill elephants like him and toucans and a crocodile, and I'd see the jungle with its mysterious light and strong winds, and I'd sit down with the elders in the meeting house, and no one would be able to say, hey you kid, don't bother your elders. And as morning wore on, I reaffirmed my soon-to-be condition of a grown-up, and I imitated the erect strut of Tío Abeso and the heavy seriousness of my father, and I had a good time imitating them with their somber voices and heroic gestures, all alone because Tía Te had disappeared after I shooed her away; I was the new man in the tribe. Because how could I be so childish as to play with little girls now that I was about to be a man?

But deep down I would have liked it never to happen, because I was scared to death. Cousin Mbo and cousin Asumu, and cousin Anton, and cousin Santos, and my friend Otunga and my friend Ba all told me many times how much it hurt, and they took and stretched my foreskin vigorously and pinched it with their nails. And when I screamed, they said, coward, if you whimper over a little joke, what will you do the day you feel a sharp machete between your legs slicing that piddling little thing right off. And I tried not to think of it, but I was already sweating a lot, and I couldn't stand it any more so I went looking for Tía Te again to ask her if she knew if it hurt much, and she said, how can I know, I'm not a man, but I've heard that what comes out of there is not pee but lots of blood. I was taken by all this and my fear doubled, and she said that to be a man is just that, blood instead of pee: men don't do it like kids, you'll see how after this afternoon you'll only pee blood, just like me when I get to be a woman, I've seen it, yes, don't look at me that way, I'm not the one who has to get cut. And she gave me a cup of the same tea my mother served me the night before, and little by little I was forgetting about the hunger that was growling in my stomach; again I felt a certain laxness, a rather dreamy feeling. But I didn't sleep. Because I went to my room and unwrapped the *clote* and spread my legs to take a look at the foreskin hanging between my thighs; gee, they're going to turn me into a man, that's what's important, and I shouldn't be afraid, you shouldn't, those cowards who won't run away when you want to give them a good punch on their wide noses, they'll have to own up to their dirty words and I'll hit them real hard, as hard as my father and Tío Abeso hit me. And when the elders arrived, they saw I was half-asleep on the bed, drooling from my lips, and my eyes were closed as I tasted future victories over cousin Mbo. And when my father woke me up with his rough voice—I don't know why but his voice sounded hoarse—I quickly got up with an eagerness that showed in my face and the way I walked, graceful and light. I could detect the figure of my mother, her face filled with tears, over there in the background inside the walls of the house, with my brother in her arms—he was only a few months old—and my sister at her feet, looking at me and smiling mischievously, and Tía Te also at her side sniveling; those little women go through life whimpering about everything and nothing; and my grandmother, Mama Fina, was strutting around sternly as if she were controlling it all. And then there'd be Tío Abeso's six wives, I think they were all there, yes, although for sure I could only pick out Mama Andeme's heavy, mournful cry, and cousin Micue's little laugh. But that treacherous Mbo was not there; he was probably playing around with his friends, I don't know, and I thanked

God for getting rid of them for me so they wouldn't make fun of me at a time like this. And there was my father with his hands crossed behind him, severe yet smiling, and Grandfather Nguema Anseme, satisfied in his ripe old age, and above all Tío Abeso who put his hand on my shoulder and led me to the door of the storage house and told me with loving sternness to sit down, and I sat down, and there was a little shallow hole in the floor right under my legs, and my father positioned himself behind me, and Tío Meco on one side and Grandfather Nguema Anseme on the other, and Tío Abeso in front of me. And Tío Abeso asked me in a tone of authority and tenderness if I had eaten anything that night, and I said no, and he asked me if I had eaten anything that morning, and I said no. Then his face turned blank; I don't know who he was looking at, because he was standing there as if he were in a trance, and then I saw the aura descend on him and how it covered his rich black body naked from the waist up; he was the only one with a bare chest. He looked left and right without seeing, because he asked my father if there was anyone else around, and my father said no, the only ones who could see us were the ones with pure eyes, or something like that, so I too looked to the left and right to see if I could find the impure eyes of some woman or an enemy of the tribe. Tío Abeso remained in his trance exalted by his mysterious magical power, and he pronounced words in a style of Fang I had never heard, and I could only figure out what he was saying when, in a monochord and fluid litany, he invoked the ancestors, even the most remote ones, those who had known the tribe in the days of the great migration through deserts, forests, and over rivers along with those who had lived on the other side of the Ntem River before the French occupiers forced the ancestor, Motulu Mbenga, to emigrate. Sacred words began to fall on my face in the form of spit, round and bubbly, and a great happiness came over me. I was acknowledged— at last!—as a legitimate descendant of the ancestors and a bona fide member of the tribe. And when Tío Abeso pronounced his own name and lodged the last loud spit on my face, the final remnant of fear fled from my body, and I saw clearly how my spirit was liberated just as my body had been liberated the night before, and I saw my soul soaring above Tío Abeso's gleaming white head, and my soul was playing with the spirits of all those ancestors I could barely make out; all I knew was that they were smiling, and from then on they took on their own makeup and personality, and I knew I would recognize them from then on wherever I found them, here, there, now, always, because they had taken me into the fold of the tribe as one of their own.

Tío Abeso bent over the pot at the feet of Grandfather Nguema Anseme and drank the thick, reddish liquid, the same as I had done a few hours ago. He rinsed his mouth with the liquid and spat it out on my cropped head, and he pronounced more words, incomprehensible to me because he spoke in such a low tone, and his voice was persuasive with all its emotion, and his words came out hushed and hesitant. All I remember is that he blessed me; he spoke of the offering to mother earth, of the blood the tribe would shed so that new lives would come from my body and from the earth, and in those lives the tribe would find new glory. And my father was the first to tie my hands behind me; I remember it perfectly, just like I remember my mother's loud cry from behind the kitchen wall at that very moment. And Grandfather Nguema Anseme and his son Tío Meco each grabbed on to one of my legs, and Tío Abeso, with infinite patience—although today I believe he was trying to hide the emotion revealed by his trembling hands—untied my *clote* and threw it far from where we were. Again he drank from the pot, rinsed his mouth, and spat on my cropped head, and before I could recover from the jolt of the liquid on my body, he grabbed and pulled the foreskin hanging between my legs and then the other hand went right for the same spot, and I felt the cut, and I felt half of it coming off, and I felt the blood flowing from my body into the mouth of mother earth. Before losing the sense of things around me in the midst of an echo of the lamentations from behind the kitchen wall, I saw Tío Abeso leaning over me, crushing a kola nut with his jaws, and hurling small bits of it on the wound between my legs.

You didn't yell or cry, remember? Not until the last drop of blood vanished into mother earth, tender and warm, reddened, inseminated by your blood, and Tío Abeso covered the hole where your blood ran forever. You didn't cry because it all occurred very fast: you could barely see the razor blade he had in his right hand when it came down quickly and cut you with one slice, an able surgeon trained by the centuries, and the little wrinkled foreskin was left in his fingers. You didn't notice it, and this is why you didn't cry, but your fame as a result of it was established for always. You were the bravest of the tribe; no child had managed to do what you did, nor would they in future generations: endure it all without shedding a single tear. And the face of Tío Abeso was filled with both satisfaction and anxiety, worried perhaps that he had cut off more than needed, and his mysterious, magical dignity and fervor were contagious, an expansive expressive energy that you would have liked to pass on to others, to those present and those who would come after you. Despite your small size, the millennial wisdom of your ancestors communicated that the event had come to pass, the mystery had been revealed to the tribe; you had been endowed with mysterious, magical power, because Tío Abeso had not only circumcised you, he had pronounced the words that admitted a new member into the tribe. Yes, but you would be a special member from then on, the second-born in an eternal lineage, and this would turn you into a sure and consecrated candidate as the transmitter of its power. He had invoked the blessing of the forefathers on you as on all the males of the tribe, and the ancestors had responded that you were no ordinary descendant, you were the one chosen to bring back the glory of the tribe; the sign of the time had manifested itself. You were one of them, and it was revealed on that sunny Sunday afternoon, and the tribe would see itself in you from then on as it saw the men predestined to carry on the tradition. When, later on, Tío Abeso looked at you intently and you held his gaze, you saw those fireflies around him and how they melded into the ones around you. They were the spirits of the dead who transmitted security, dignity, and strength to you; this was necessary so that the tribe should see you as a firm and just chief. You understood it clearly. And Abeso knew it well, the only one who could know it; only he could transmit those qualities, only he could choose and recommend. And as the last drop fell into the earth, the air penetrated your body for the first time and you let out a yell, bold, human, hopeful—the yell Tío Abeso was waiting for to assure the perfection of his mission, the yell your father too awaited, absorbed in your convulsions, his eyes fixed on Tío Abeso. And above all it was the yell your mother was waiting for because it told her everything had come out all right; like the first yell of your life, it was received happily through tears mounting in her eyes. And everything was consummated. Your convulsions, your kicks, the sting of the open wound, the animal flexions of your thighs and buttocks despite the iron grip of Grandfather Nguema Anseme's hands, Tío Meco too: the unlocked doors to the wound broke open again and the bleeding resumed. But you no longer saw the blood because it had disappeared into the blood already shed into mother earth; your eyes were flooded and your head turned back, toward your father who held you with all his strength. So they carried you off, and you squirmed like a captured baby gorilla (determined to die fighting, resisting bravely and defiantly). The procession began slowly toward the banana groves, and as you passed the kitchen wall, the cries of your mother and grandmother were mixed with your own, and you called for your mother—mommy, come save me!—and they smiled in their tears, and she couldn't save you because she knew your salvation depended on that slow pilgrimage toward the banana grove. And you knew it too, they knew it, and everyone knew it, but you were only a six-year-old child—Was it six?—and the pain was sharp where the open wound throbbed between your thighs. And when you arrived at the banana grove, Tío Abeso knelt beside a bush in the corner and dug a little hole with his hands; he spread his saliva over it, purifying, animating, bits of kola nuts still protruding from the hole. He pronounced some words you couldn't understand because you were still sobbing, but it didn't matter, for the words were directed to the tribe, not to you; you could only see him there kneeling down at the edge of the banana grove, his bare torso white at the nape of his neck. And Grandfather Nguema Anseme joined him, and he too pronounced some unintelligible words, his eyes fixed on the wrinkled bit of flesh deposited in the hole next to Tío Abeso by the banana trees. And when they both arose, they joined hands and pronounced more words looking right at you. By this time you weren't crying any more, just whimpering; you understood what they were saying, and you will never forget: the two tribes that had given you their life were bestowing on you a boundless confidence, a confidence you would merit in the future because of your loyalty to the tribe—obeying and respecting the elders, upholding tradition, being prudent and brave, strict and generous, watching out for the well-being of your people, always mindful, unflinching in the face of enemies, legitimating the power conferred by the ancestors. Grandfather Nguema Anseme spat three times into the hole at the edge of the banana grove, cursing the women who dared step on that sacred earth or who took the liberty of eating the fruit of your seed and then cursing the evil spirits who projected themselves on you and any living thing that might harm you or defy the power of the dead. You gladly accepted the mandate of the tribes; don't deny it now, no matter how old you are, in spite of the intense pain between your legs, and remember they asked you three times if you were a defender of the traditions of your people. Three times they asked you if you would run away in the face of enemies, and you answered that you would never flee in the face of enemies of the tribe, and another three times they asked you if you would muster the strength and courage necessary to live the hard life of a man on earth, and you responded that you would know how to muster the strength necessary to live the life of a man on earth. And as they rubbed the mixture into your body for the last time, Tío Abeso and Grandfather Nguema Anseme gave you their respective names, the names by which you would be known by those around you, the ascendants and descendants of each of the lineages. And you received the alligator's tooth and the turtle's skull, clear symbols of your bloodline, signs of wisdom and honor, love and strength, valor and prudence, the horizons of your desires and the limits of your power over the tribe. Throughout a process you thought had begun a few days earlier as the result of a little quarrel but had really begun many months before and would last for many years to come (even though you didn't know it), you were able to grasp your own self as a person, no longer subject to the uselessness of childhood. It all left a permanent gap in your soul, and you were consecrated from then on to acquire the necessary merits for the acclamation of the tribe. You were aware of the change going on in your small body, yes, even though eroding whispers relegated them to the corners of your mind: only an ascendance to a superior state, the state that would define you as guardian of your people against intruders, against those of bad faith, against the cowardly and inept. Because all those would be denied access to the relics and secrets of the tribe; continuity, unity, and abundance would not be known by the enemies. This alone would now be your life; it would be kept secure and vigilant against failure and weakness.

And that night—remember?—you saw your great-grandfather, Motulu Mbenga, for the first time, founder of your family line and upholder of tribal customs, on the banks of the Ntem River. Your great-grandfather was standing on an alligator floating on the water, barely visible from where you were sitting on a large rock painted white and red on the shore of the great river, and the great-grandfather's feet were dry. On the opposite bank you saw some phantasmagorical figures, grotesque little humanoids with rifles spitting out fire and iron at your great-grandfather, and they were getting drunk from leather containers filled with that liquid that burns your throat, and they had chips of mirror and strings of beads wrapped around their hands. And the shots didn't reach your great-grandfather; he moved his hand to his majestic head to brush away some insects that looked to you like black flies. And the insects swarmed around him and went back to the opposite riverbank and then crawled into the tubes vomiting fire and iron. But the shots ceased, and the insects began to gnaw at the tubes and handles and at the arms, chest, stomach, and face of the attackers. And in a few moments the humanoids were reduced to ghostly skeletons with no eyes and a pith helmet dancing on their long golden skulls. The alligator then emerged from the water and delivered Great-grandfather Motulu Mbenga to the bank, and then a meadow, vast, flat, and filled with flowers, appeared in front of you. And in the middle, a path that led to a cabin outlined far away on the horizon, and in front of the house a gigantic *ekuk* tree with four branches as thick as its own trunk pointing north, south, east, and west. You closely followed Great-grandfather Motulu Mbenga with your eyes, and as he reached the gigantic *ekuk,* he turned back and stared at you with his eyes as radiant as the morning sun, and he took you by the hand. And you both made rings around the gigantic *ekuk* until an ax fell from the branch that pointed north, and from the one pointing south came the alligator's skin, from the one pointing east came fire, and from the westward branch came a turtle. And before your eyes appeared a long procession of humanoids who had been turned into skeletons from the waist up, still dressed in worn Caribbean-style shirts and carrying the rusty rifles eaten away by the insects. And a naked old woman came out of the house, her face tattooed with symbols of wisdom, and she pointed to the branch facing west, and you saw the turtle hanging there, and the turtle disappeared into your head. And you were anointed with prudence, and the woman touched her genitals and mouth at the same time: always close the door and your mouth along with it, and when you travel, always listen for things from behind. She then turned toward the branch facing east and the flame grew larger only to be put out an instant later. And you were then anointed with the necessary strength, and the woman brought her hand to her heart and said, just as the antelope is not the offspring of the elephant, when you hear that it has arrived, think of it as leaving. And turning to the south-pointing branch where the alligator's skin had disappeared, the old woman brought her hands to her feet and gave you temperance, and as you grew on the inside you heard these words: the gazelle lives in the prairies, the buffalo in the brambles, and man in his town. And when she looked north, the ax came down and landed in your right hand and justice entered your spirit. And the woman gazed into your eyes and said, even though you may have a wife in the future, you must learn to cook, because life has many surprises, and don't cry, don't cry! because crying is the last thing. And Great-grandfather Motulu Mbenga asked you what you were looking for there, and you answered that you were looking for him, and he said, I am you, don't you see? and you saw yourself alone with the ax in your hand in the middle of the tribe. Your great-grandfather had disappeared, the old woman had disappeared, the gigantic *ekuk* had disappeared, the meadow had disappeared along with the cabin. And all the tribe acclaimed you because there in the earth, spread out on the main street of the village, were the skeletons of the humanoids, and the insects were crawling out from the hollows of their eyes and from the mouths of their rifles.

And well before dawn during the five weeks that followed, Tío Abeso took me to the river. We left when it was still dark and before the cocks began to crow in the patio; we were dressed the same, each with a white *clote* tied at the neck covering our entire bodies. He had a cane in his right hand, and my uncle took his time as he strolled purposefully and slowly because I couldn't walk fast enough; the wound between my thighs still hurt, and the swelling had reached my groin. He would whistle a song now and then, or he would frighten away a nocturnal animal that crossed our path, or he would help me along when the pain or sleepiness wouldn't allow me to continue, but I couldn't stop, I knew it, we had to keep on walking without stopping until we got to the riverbank. Then he took off my white *clote* and gathered it into a bunch and stepped carefully; then he put it on the white sand, and we kept on going into the water over the slippery rocks against the current. But I couldn't fall, I knew it, for we were moving slowly because we could barely see, morning having not yet arrived. We sat down on the big rock in the middle of the bed of the wide river at the foot of the waterfall. And I could see the pure white bubbling foam from the stream of water falling from high up into the river and getting into the spaces between my toes, each pellet of water like thick drops of dew sprinkled on my body, and Tío Abeso, too, was at my side, and we stayed there a long time, contemplating the waterfall and the black waters shining, and the sky was clear and red, the scene of the last battle between light and darkness. We didn't speak because we would not have been able to understand one another, although I always suspected that my uncle was speaking to someone because he was absorbed in contemplating the deep waters, or perhaps he was looking at the clear light coming down from the clouds and wounding the dew rolling over the river. And when the first rays of sun came through the dark waters and reflected our bodies in a water-soaked mirror, Tío Abeso stood up and helped me stand up.

We abandoned the spot where we were and proceeded downstream to the whirling waters, the place where the river was compensated for its work by the drowning of two members of the tribe each year. And Tío Abeso dunked me into the water; he was standing on the slippery shiny rock holding me under my arms. I noticed how my body was seized by the whirling waters in that spot; Tío Abeso had to make an effort not to slip on the rock, fighting against the rolling waters, and my cries were drowned by the echo of the cascade and the roar of the waters, and by the intense fear of sinking in the middle of a black lagoon and never coming up, and the gripping cold of the morning freezing and numbing my lower body parts until I could no longer feel them, and the sweat on the face of Tío Abeso, transfigured as he spat into my face, his words meant to drive out evil spirits along with my fear as he prayed for the ancestors' blessing and the tribe's respect. And when, in a supreme effort with all the force of my six short years, I hoisted myself up out of the deep whirling water, I suddenly felt an intense heat in my buttocks, my legs, and my belly and a light shiver, perhaps due to the fear and the cold and the hunger, and I saw the sun shining from on top of the waterfall. And I thought life was beautiful, and the warm rays of sun shone down on my wound, suddenly clean, as Tío Abeso spat bits of kola nuts on it. And with all the care and delicacy in the world, he took out a paste of boiled leaves from the folds of his *clote* and wrapped the tip of my foreskin in it. At first it burned, but later, when the color became more black than red, it soothed the sting of the water.

The last night after five weeks of ablutions every morning, I found myself in the center of a tribal gathering on Tío Abeso's patio. It was a clear, calm night, a large moon shone in all its glory in the heart of a limpid black sky, circled by the resplendent glow of the clouds. I was in the first row, sitting at the feet of Tío Abeso whose breathing pumped a prominent belly, and I could feel the slow rhythm of his belly as it compressed and swelled against my cropped head, that regular rhythm, steady, yearning, became one with my own. It was the prelude to the pulsations of the night; it accompanied me later and flooded my spirit with its force and tenderness. My father was sitting with the distinguished members of the tribe far away from me, and he looked at me, all serious, with that stern look that only he can give me. And I wondered if he would like the ceremony that was about to begin, but I would never know because his face never expressed anything, no emotion, no fear, no satisfaction, no dissatisfaction. Grandfather Nguema Anseme, sitting, close to Tío Abeso, looked at me from time to time and smiled, grabbing my hand and squeezing it in his own rough, wrinkled hands, but he said nothing. And all the eyes of the tribe were on me, still dressed in the white sheet, even though the wound had healed and my foreskin now was just like cousin Mbe's. It had even taken the same shape as Tío Abeso's—a healthy red and sticking out; I'd seen it when we were in the river five weeks ago, those five weeks that had ended forever—although mine was smaller, of course. And I was pleased with myself, safe and happy, because now I was a man for the tribe, and I was a man for myself. And the women: what a handsome boy he is, he's almost as tall as Papa Abeso; and they touched me and stroked me and rubbed my cropped head with palm oil mixed with brilliantine. Tío Abeso stood up and made me stand up with him, he looked to one side of the plaza then to the other without seeing anything, because he asked if there was anyone else among us. And the tribe said no, that we could only be seen with pure eyes; and the circle was getting wider, the moon was the only light, the shadows shivered in the warm night, but nothing made me afraid, not even the hundreds of pairs of eyes looking at me from between the shadows, because I knew they were confident eyes filled with the love and hope of the whole tribe, and those eyes were fixed on mine. Tío Abeso asked if there was anyone who felt they were more qualified than he to sit in the chair protected by the alligator. And no one spoke; the silence was as heavy as the wind blowing through the ghostly dark trees of the forest close by; the only sound was the cough of a child behind us from where the women were. Tío Abeso asked if the tribe still considered him their leader, and all responded in unison that Bulu Abeso Motulu was the only leader, and no one disputed this because he was still the benevolent and just leader chosen by the great Abeso Motulu. Tío Abeso, with his lofty, magical dignity, then asked if the entire tribe was present, and all answered that the tribe was present. The only one missing was Mico Ondo, who was dying and whose spirit is with us along with the spirits of the ancestors. And Tío Abeso's voice was like something I would never hear again, grave, powerful, rough, persuasive, and emphatic. He asked if those present respected his decision to confer this direct descendant of Motulu Mbenga, born a male and deemed a man, and to initiate him into the secrets of the tribe. And all responded that both those present and those absent respected the decision made by Chief Bulu Abeso Motulu if this is the will of the great Mutulo Mbenga. And at that moment he spat three times on my cropped head and intoned a sad and melodious song followed along by a chorus from the women sitting behind us. A path was opened in front of us, and between the shadows the figure of an old woman emerged, naked from the waist up with her flaccid breasts hanging on her stomach, her arms painted red with the liquid of the *bea* plant and her torso white with the liquid of the *ekuuan*, and in one hand she had a bow and in the other an ax, and monkey fur covered her shoulders, and bracelets and amulets encircled her arms, and seeds tinkling like bells and lines of dry leaves were around her waist and legs; her head decorated with abundant colorful feathers, and her face was covered by a mask I had never seen and would never see again. When the *akoma* woman—years later I learned that it was Grandmother Mama Fina, the first wife of Tío Abeso—spoke somberly, praising the tribe and its will to resist, she was constantly reinforced by the chorus behind us and accompanied by the rhythmic, hollow beat of the *tumba* played by my cousin Paco. She was in a frenzy: she looked like a little girl, so flexible, her hips gyrating with her hands, her feet not touching the ground, her head rotating, and her mask always staring at me even though she had her back to me. I don't know how she did it, but that's the way I saw it, and she threw herself down and remained in a convulsive ecstasy, and the night was filled with the beat of cousin Paco's drumsticks bringing out emotions that had been sleeping deep within the tribe. And the old woman was writhing on the ground, and little by little she arose, rhythmically, with her hips, breasts, arms, and the mask on her head always in motion, and she moved to the cadences of the *tumba* accompanied by hundreds of hands clapping. And she passed the ax on to another woman also dressed colorfully, the only difference being that her shoulders were covered by alligator skin; and when I heard her voice, I knew it was my mother, and a lively urge came over me to follow her naked feet on the dusty ground, her strident song interspersed with yelps of joy and cries breaking the night. And my cousin Paco was more inspired than ever, beating away at his *tumba* with the wisdom of his fingers communicating the jubilation of our tribe to all the friendly tribes nearby, and to the enemy tribes he conveyed the will to resist, but they would never know it. And my mother handed over the ax to Tío Abeso's first wife, Mama Andeme gave it to the second, the second to the third, and so on, continuously singing and dancing with new songs, continuously dancing. Her voice will always be in my memory, like her words; they gave thanks to the ancestors for not having abandoned the tribe, and they sang the glorious death of Chief Abeso Motulu at the hands of the occupiers. They celebrated the future victories of the children of the tribe, and they glorified the end of servitude for future generations. They told my mother—who was now at the center of the dance, after my grandmother, surely exhausted by all the activity, had stepped out—that from her womb a descendant of Motulu Mbenga had been born who would bring the tribe into a new land filled with flowers and love. And where there would be abundance, the children would grow, the blood of the women would not run dry, the alligators would not attack the men, and the tribe would find new glory. Far away, in the dark, mysterious night, tenuously lit by a rising moon, birds began to chirp: pronouncements, wants, accomplishments, and the premonitions of the tribe. Dancing shadows covered me, all of us, and the trees and the insects and the animals looked at us expectantly, paralyzed by the loud beat of the *tumba* along with the hearts and muscles of the tribe. Then I knew the night would no longer frighten me, since I could recognize its noises and shadows, and my will was much stronger than the yelps of the monkeys or the roar of the lion or the scurry of the genet or the cry of the gorilla or the hiss of the boa whose skin covered the backs of the dancers, all symbols of my triumph over the fears of the tribe. And the dance continued throughout the night, with a few interruptions so that the women could drink water from a container made out of a pumpkin to compensate for the sweat that was drenching their black torsos painted red and white. For an affliction was hanging over the tribe, a great affliction encircling the moon, a huge moon, a warm, sacred image of my ancestral strength that would guide me through dark nights and lead me here, there, then, always, until the goal was realized and prosperity returned to the tribe. And when the voices softened and the lively sound of the *tumba* was lowered, after my grandmother had set the bow down in front of me pointing downward, its arc taut, I rose, picked it up, went over to the edge of the banana trees, stuck the arrow in the red circle, and buried my childhood forever. Tío Abeso lifted me up on his shoulders, the bow firmly in my hands, and we went into the shadows of the jungle. The tribe then dispersed behind us, the moon was still encased in a dark sky reigning over the living and the dead, and out of nothing the path was opening before me. I never thought there was a trail there, and Tío Abeso walked swiftly as if I didn't weigh anything, and the moon disappeared behind the treetops, and the night revealed itself to us, dark and gloomy. The spirits continued dancing in the thickness, and the birds had stopped chirping, and the animals had gone to sleep, silenced by fear and alarmed by the magical and mysterious power emanating from the figure of Tío Abeso; there were no animals other than an owl hooting mournfully from the mysterious tree of knowledge, but I was no longer afraid of anything. The morning dew on my head drenching my white *clote* kept me fully awake, vigilant, infected by the strength and valor of Tío Abeso, who kept on walking and walking, opening the trail of nothingness, without direction, I thought, because we circled the gigantic *ekuk* tree with the four branches pointing in the four directions. And I thought we had gotten lost because we kept on circling the gigantic *ekuk* with the branches pointing in the four directions again and again and round and round, and the branch pointing north looked dry to me, and the one pointing south disappeared at that moment, and my uncle also saw it, but he didn't say anything, he just kept making circles around the gigantic *ekuk*. And once he stumbled over a root coming out of the earth, and the branch pointing east was broken by a lightning flash, and its sap dripped onto my eyes, and then I saw it too, following the line of the branch pointing west, majestic and solid, brilliant and real: an adobe cabin appeared in the middle of a beautiful, large opening with dew-covered flowers. And at the door there was a very old woman who looked blind to me; she asked Tío Abeso what he wanted to see in all that darkness, and Tío Abeso answered that there was no darkness in the dwelling of the dead. The woman approached us, slowly, groping carefully through the cool air, as if she were afraid of falling. She came closer to us, drawn by the voice of Tío Abeso and the mournful hooting of the owl on top of the gigantic *ekuk* on the branch pointing west. She repeated her question and my uncle repeated his answer, and the woman asked if the little boy on his shoulders also saw the light, and I said indeed, that I saw lots of light, that it was not night here because everything was brilliantly lit. The old woman asked what I saw, and my voice sounded loud and metallic when I responded that I saw her all wrinkled and her eyes closed; they were the kind of eyes that oozed a whitish liquid, and I saw a passageway with flowers all of different colors, and the horizon at the end of it; there was a marvelous cabin with just one door and no windows. The old woman then knelt down, grabbed Tío Abeso's hands, and licked them, and when she had finished, my uncle gently put me down, and I held his hand, and the woman held my other hand and said to us, follow me, my fathers, to your dwelling. And the cabin was illuminated by the sparkling glow of the moon, and the air was cool, and the sweet smell of the flowers overtook everything, and the entire cabin was filled with bows and arrows and harps and *tumba*s and amulets and masks; farther on, on an upper level supported by four columns, I could see the skulls of the ancestors. Tío Abeso knelt down, and I did the same; he did not say anything, he only looked at the hollows of the nonexistent eyes in the skulls, ten, twenty, I don't know how many, and I also looked at them stupefied, and I was seized by an unspeakable fear. My hands began to sweat, the old woman licked them clean, and the fear went away. The place was beautiful, a celestial beauty, and the skulls of the chiefs began to speak to me, their toothless jaws moving up and down without saying anything I could understand no matter how much I tried. And my uncle stood there, calm, possessed as usual by his mysterious, magical dignity. And the old woman approached me with something in her hands, a bowl made from a pumpkin, saying, drink, dear father, and I drank what was in the bowl, it was sweet, very sweet, and I gave the bowl back to the old woman, and the old woman brought another pumpkin bowl. There was just one kola nut, and she told me to eat it, O father of mine, and I ate it and it was bitter, very bitter. And then I heard the voice of Great-grandfather Motulu Mbenga, and I saw his face on the upper level of the cabin, and he told Tío Abeso to rub the medicine over my neck and face, and the face of chief Abeso Motulu told me that I was about to be anointed with the potion that would give power to the tribe, and that it would endow me with the strength to confront the enemies and regain the tribe's glory. And all the heads of all the other chiefs of our clan sang a war song, and I heard the distinct beats of the *tumba* calling for war, and cousin Paco was at my side, not there but in the future, holding the drumsticks between his teeth and dipping the points of the lances in poison as the whole tribe began to dance. My uncle rose and went to the upper level, where the faces of the ancestors were, and he grabbed a dissected boa and took some powder out of its mouth; and as the old woman made small incisions in the nape of my neck and on my face with her sharp black nails, Tío Abeso cured my little wounds with the powder he had taken from the mouth of the boa. Again the face of Motulu Mbenga spoke, telling my uncle to cut a piece of the bone that he had tied to his waist. And for the first time I knew that Tío Abeso had a bone tied to his waist, and my great-grandfather ordered that he carefully wrap the chip of bone, and my uncle did as he was told, and they gave me the wrapped chip of bone, and Great-grandfather Motulo Mbenga told me to keep the wrapped bone chip in a place that only I could remember; and when you want to be near us, put the chip under your tongue and you will always find your way out of nothingness to our dwelling. And when the old woman opened the door again and left us under the gigantic *ekuk*, she disappeared, everything disappeared: the passageway, the flowers. And the horizon swallowed up the beautiful adobe cabin, and I found myself next to Tío Abeso sitting at the base of the gigantic *ekuk*, which was completely petrified, its four branches pointing in four directions in the middle of my father's coffee plantation. The bow was resting at my feet but without the arrow, the dew was drenching my white *clote*, my feet ached terribly, as if I had been walking for a long time. I rubbed my face and neck and I felt no pain, nor any sign of my wound, and the sun shone brilliantly in a blue sky, intensely blue. And my father's rifle was resting at the feet of Tío Abeso, and next to it a black and white toucan with its three beaks stuck in the ground.

tħree

When I was eight, I knew Father Claret's catechism by heart, and my favorite book was his *Straight and Sure Path to Heaven*. The horror of eternal condemnation didn't allow me to be a child. I didn't go to the Wele River with Ba any more, I couldn't learn how to make those bamboo toy cars that I loved so much even though cousin Asumu offered to teach me many times. I didn't carve arrows to shoot at birds anymore, I didn't go swimming in the Nganga River with my friend Otunga or my cousins Anton and Mbo. Even today I don't know how to swim. I didn't have a hunting dog, and I didn't know how to make a cage for trapping fish. All this was for other children now, for the ones who weren't fortunate enough to be touched by the grace of God. What's the use of all that fun and idleness if in the end your soul is damned forever? Father Claret, the saintly one, asked me this as I read his book, and I had no choice; I had to acknowledge that the most important part of my life was my soul, and to be saved I had to avoid useless amusements, the silly games of my friends, my cousins, the brothers in my tribe. It was shortly before I was nine when I got into the habit of saying Mass from a little altar I made for myself in my room in front of the crucifix Father Ortiz had given me and under the religious things I had on the wall: the Eye-of-God triangle and some prints that were brought to me by my father's white friends; the *Little Prayer Book* served as missal. Alone in my room, when no one was looking, when my little brothers succumbed to the midday sun, I got all dressed up in a bed sheet and pretended it was a priest's chasuble and started to say Mass, *in nomine Patris et Filii et Spritus Sancti*, and I made the sign of the cross: I, a sinner, confess to Almighty God and the Blessed Mary Ever Virgin, Saint Michael the Archangel, John the Baptist, and to Apostles Peter and Paul and all the saints, and I beat my little breast in contrition, *mea culpa, mea culpa, mea maxima culpa*, and I almost forgot the *kyrie eleison kyrie eleison Christe eleison Christe eleison*, then the *introito, oremus*, and I turned my head ceremoniously; then in silent fervor I genuflected, *gloria in excelsis Deo*, and I recited it all without knowing what I said in a Latin I learned from listening to Father Ortiz so much. And I turned to the parishioners; they were all pleased with me, *dominus voviscum et cum espiritu tuo, oremus*, and I turned to the *Little Prayer Book*, which I had propped against a rock, pretending it was a lectern so that the missal would be in its proper place. And I turned to the page I had marked with a red ribbon I had snatched from my mother's closet; it was the Epistle to the Corinthians, I knew it almost by heart, and I kissed the altar, genuflected, *in illo tempore dixit Iesu discipulis suis*, Saint Mark, chapter five, verses two to ten. Then, carefully, I kissed the substitute missal and turned ceremoniously as if I were illuminated: dear brethren, you who have come here to this temple of holy sacrifice to hear the gospel, and I spoke the word of God to these imaginary parishioners, and the meaning of the mystery of Incarnation, how God the Father sent his only Son to save us, especially heathens like us, how we flagellated the Lord like the Jews of old with our barbaric customs, our lust for riches, coveting what others have when Christ promised heaven to the poor; the only richness pleasing to the eyes of God is that of the soul, a white and pure soul, and I reminded my sheep of the parable of the reaper, and that I hoped a seed would fall on the good earth and bear fruit in those afflicted hearts, or the one about the prodigal son, hoping that those who strayed from the flock of the divine Redeemer would come back to him in repentance. You should know that Epulon, the rich man, is now burning in hell for eternity while poor Lazarus, so unfortunate in this valley of tears, is now in the lap of God. God loves the poor, the humble; Christ declared it unequivocally in his infinite wisdom, it is easier for a camel to pass through the eye of a needle than for a rich man to enter my Father's kingdom: now you know why one must not covet others' goods; suffering awaits the rich in the next life because God is just to all; he delivers the deserved reward and to each one of us a place on earth and in heaven from which we should serve him despite our poverty and wretchedness, for eternal glory awaits us, and only if we serve him gladly are we worthy of his infinite mercy.

These words resounded in my room and echoed reverentially throughout the house—our zinc roof still did not cover it completely—and an apostolic yearning came over me, and I was determined to fulfill our Lord's mandate to the disciples: go and preach the Gospel to all in the world; where two people are united in my name, I will be there with you; and I felt like Peter: the stone, the rock on which the Church of my people would be edified, that it not disappear until the end of time.

Like Father Ortiz, I didn't see the many eyes scrutinizing me from below, with their black faces listening to me without understanding, and like the priest, I asked myself if those people were actually capable of grasping the wise teachings I tried to impart from the pulpit of my bed. With the priest, I asked myself if all those dirty, smelly blacks, no matter that they were dressed in their Sunday best, if those poor folk devoured by mosquitoes, reduced to a hypnotic, irreversible state by dysentery and malaria, always looking lethargic, dazed, submissive, if only those men, women, and children, so dim-witted, so attached to the savage nature surrounding them, were worthy of the immense goodness I was trying to bring them as I offered the possibility of a new life, eternal life, *amen, per omnia secula seculoreum,* trying to rid them of their idolatry and elevating them to the supreme category of civilized beings. A mystical doubt assaulted me, and with humility I acknowledged God's response; indeed, that doubt was the source of my faith. I felt I had been chosen, and I declared my conviction to carry out such a lofty mission. I enjoyed reminding my imaginary congregants of the resurrection of Lazarus,

Christ curing lepers and people plagued by dropsy, but leprosy was not only in the body; I would tell them that the worst leprosy is in the soul. And I said this with such fervor that I was certain a seed would find its way to fertile ground, and then my work would be fully justified: on the day of the resurrection of the flesh, when the angels would lift us from our tombs with their glorious trumpets in all their celestial rhythm, I would find myself at the right hand of God, among the just, because I would have contributed to the conversion of wretched lost souls, I would have helped forge Eden on this barren earth.

And reverently I returned to the altar, turning my back to my repentant sheep as they knelt down noisily, *credo in unum Deum Pater ominipotente factorem coeli et terrae visivilium et invisibilium et Domine Iesu Christi Filius Dei Unigenitus*—pause to take a breath—*Deus de Deo lumen de lumine Deus verus de Deo Vero*—another rest, I had to swallow. With maximum faith and filled with emotion, I got back on track, *genitus non factus, est qui propter*; I forgot a few words, but I continued with renewed enthusiasm, this time without hesitation, *descendit de coeli et incarnatus est de spiritu sancto et Maria Virgine*, and I kept on reciting what I thought was Latin without knowing exactly what I was saying, whatever came into my head just as it came out of Father Ortiz's mouth, *et homo factus est crucifixus etiam pro nobis sub Pontio Pilato passus et sepultus est*. I was seized by the happiness of the glorious resurrection on the third day, as the scriptures told it, *ascendit in coelis desux ad dexteram Patris et iterum venturus est cum gloria iudicare vivos et mortuos cuius regnum non erit finis*; I believed in the Holy Spirit, Lord and giver of life *qui ex Pa-ter Filioque procedit*, who received all the glory and adoration, and I believed in Holy Mother the Church without question, holy and apostolic, and in the communion of saints and in life everlasting. Amen. I dipped my fingers in pretend holy water, I dabbed them dry in an automatic gesture with a white napkin, I mixed water with water in a container I called a chalice, I genuflected, *dominus vobiscum et cum spiritu tuo sursum cordam habemus a Domine*, I took a little dish I prepared with finely cut slices of banana, and I whispered the words of the consecration, just as softly as Father Ortiz; and lifting the banana plate up toward the zinc roof, I made the bells ring in my head, and they rang and I genuflected, the same as in the last supper; he took the chalice, I took it, he blessed it, I blessed it, and he gave it to his disciples saying, *hoc est calix sanguinis meis novi et aeterni testamenti misterium fidei*; I lowered my voice even more, and I raised the container of water with water toward the roof as I listened to the bells in my head; I genuflected, I extended my arms, I turned my head toward the *Little Prayer Book*, I turned to the page with the red ribbon, and I mumbled words loosely mimicking those I distinctly heard from Father Ortiz. At this point, just like Father Ortiz, I sped up the ceremony; I turned the pages of the pretend missal, I lip-read the words, I uncovered the container of water, I covered it again with the folded napkin, I bended my knee quickly without touching the floor, *oremus, pater noster qui est in coelis sanctificatur nomen tuum adveniat regnum tuum fiat voluntas tuas*. And leaning over the night table I had turned into an altar, I beat my breast profusely, *sancto,*

sancto, sancto, and I uncovered the little plate of banana slices, and with utmost fervor and devotion, I placed all of them in my mouth and dissolved them with my tongue against my palate without chewing; I uncovered the container/chalice, I poured water into the water pretending it was wine and took a sip of the water with water, I swallowed, and then I drank the entire contents, tilting my head backwards. I dabbed my lips with the napkin as I cleared the tray, then I crushed the remaining slices of banana into the water container, filled it up again with water mixed with water, and drank it again, tilting my head backwards. I dried the container, still clearing the tray, and folded the napkin carefully, *oremus*, murmuring, looking at the *Little Prayer Book* from the corner of my eye, *dominus vobiscum et cum spiritu tuo, pax vobis, benedicat vos omnipotem Deus, Pater et Filii et spiritu sancti*, and turning to my imaginary parishioners I made the sign of the cross for them with four fingers of my right hand straight and my thumb bended at the palm, my left hand on my heart. I was filled with pride and humility, *descendant super vos et maneat semper, ite misa est, Deo gratias*.

And then I felt content, fortunate; I snuffed out the candles, undressed with decorum, gathered together the wine vessel and the paten and the chalice, and put everything in its place so that no one would know where they had been, and I said to myself that the only thing I wanted in this life was to be a priest: to save my soul from eternal damnation and do everything I could to protect my people from eternal torment, especially those who had not received the message of Revelation. I knew that my godfather approved of the idea, from the right hand of the Virgin Mary up there on high between the wide blue clouds, and I was sure my father would be delighted. But I didn't know how I would tell him.

Since leaving the seminary, I tremble each time I receive a letter from my father. My mother and father are deeply disappointed that I've abandoned my wish to be a priest. I wrote a long and thoughtful letter explaining my decision. They don't understand it. They've said so in a long and thoughtful letter. My father, in all his caustic and vexing crudeness, describes in great detail how my mother didn't stop crying for weeks after receiving my letter. My father doesn't speak of his own feelings, although I imagine he cried too. He threw a terrible question at me: Could he ever trust me again now that I have a history of not keeping a promise? Having a priest for a son is what's most important to them, their generation, the generation that came of age at the point of achieving political independence without understanding the meaning of liberty. Priests, for them, represent all human and divine knowledge. They don't understand that I've entered law school, that I actually want to be a lawyer. What's that? I open the letter with little enthusiasm; something slips out of the envelope postmarked from Bata. He always does it that way. After wishing me perfect health and telling me that the family is in good health, he goes on to explain that he is planting cocoa in the new plantation, that cocoa is the product of the future, and you always have to be prepared for the future.

Your little brother Bon has begun to study with Tío Meco; the others are in Bata, with the Brethren of La Salle, and the little ones are in town. Don Ramón is no longer here, they moved him somewhere else, and all of us are saddened that you no longer wish to be a priest. This is a wound that will take a long time to heal, my son, and you might send us more photos of yourself in the new way you dress, because now that you have given up on the priesthood, your mother and I find it impossible to look at the photos we have without suffering. Worse is that when everyone asks about you, saying they want to see you, it's not right that we have to show a picture of you dressed in a cassock if you don't wear it any more. Miguel Oyono's son cut his finger working on his land, that's the only news. Everyone is well, be a good boy, my son, keep on praying hard, God will forgive you and encourage you in his infinite mercy. Don't run around with women, don't bring us home a white woman, your mother wouldn't be able to handle that. We know that in the world you're living in now, with no one to protect you, that's very dangerous. Don't let yourself be fooled by passing illusions, your country always comes first and your family too, the family you left here because you wanted to finish your studies to become a priest, and now it looks like you want to spend more time in Spain. Think of our sacrifices, take care, my son, study, study what you want, but always strive to be an honorable man and write to us, your father who loves you. And he signed his name along with my mother's.

Always reproaching me. I suppose it was when I was nine that my father discovered how I enjoyed pretending to say Mass when I was alone. One day he came home early from working on the plantation and saw me performing my priestly duties, and I was very nervous wondering what he was going to say. Normally he would hit me and knock me to the floor, breaking the dirty dishes, and my little brother crying and no one attending to him, and there you are with all this foolishness offending God; you're the oldest so you have to set an example, take care of your little brothers and sisters just like your mother and I take care of you, and don't offend God because God will offend you for saying his name in vain and he will punish me. And I would have nothing to say as usual; I wouldn't answer. No one said anything to my father when he was mad; it was like a bee flying around your ear and you couldn't do anything about it; do something about it; keep yourself busy, don't cross your arms, a man can't go through the whole day without doing anything, "idleness is the mother of all vices" (he would say in his African-inflected Spanish), and we would look at him like zombies, not daring to move until he told us to do something, get the broom, go to the river for water, your mother is very tired, she has to bring us the water no matter how tired she is, and you just sit there with your mouths open for the flies to get in, you don't do anything useful the whole day, from the minute you get out of school all you do is wait to be fed, "those who don't work don't eat"; I've told you not to eat at other people's houses, only eat the food at your own house, only the meals at this house and only this house, there's a lot of witchcraft out there, and the snake charmers could give you human flesh and bewitch you, don't leave the patio, here you're safe from the people who want to bother you when we're here, you don't know about life, there are people who cast spells over children and kill them and eat them in their nighttime ceremonies and then force you to kill us, what will happen, whose fault will that be, let this be a warning, there's a lot of witchcraft around here, black witchcraft, it only causes death, white people also have their witchcraft but they perform it in the light of day, it produces clothes, cars, airplanes, canned sardines in olive oil that you like so much, bicycles and lots of things, don't say I didn't warn you, I have fulfilled my fatherly obligation by warning you, you in turn must fulfill your obligation as obedient children, wipe your nose, you look like a grunting pig, your mother and I suffer when you disobey, a child must obey his mother and father, that is the law of God, honor your father and mother (in his African Spanish), and don't pay any attention to anyone, I made this fence for you, don't trust anyone except your mommy and dad, no one comes here to bring you food or more clothes except your mother and me, we only ask that you obey, if they offer you something out there first ask us before you eat it, even if a piece of candy smells good that doesn't mean it's not poison, there are many people who don't like that others are well off, they're envious, envy is the first weakness of the black people, be humble, pride offends God, all of us have what we have because God helps those who help themselves, this is not boasting, where are your *wambas*, go put them on right away, you'll cry when the chiggers get into you and your fingers swell up, you come with me to harvest the coffee, looks like it's going to rain, move faster, you're as slow as snails with no legs, be careful, look at that one's face, looks like she doesn't like to work, if you don't like to work how will you live when I'm not here the day the Lord calls me, everything that I've done is not enough for the big family the Lord has given me, that's why you'll have to work and study, study hard because the future world will be governed by geniuses, wise men, another kind of wise man, not the old ones, work and study hard to be honorable and productive, work makes man worthy, the Lord said so, you will eat by the sweat of your brow. And he brought his right forefinger to the left side of his face and very slowly rubbed his wrinkles, all the way to his right ear. Then, shaking his finger vigorously as if to rid himself of huge drops of sweat that looked to me like they were thick drops of his dark red blood, your poor mother bending over the earth from dawn to dusk, planting yucca, picking peanuts, gathering bananas, grinding *bambucha*, planting yams, cutting down palm trees all for you, and all of you like idiots take it for granted, all the effort and work, all the sacrifice you're costing, and when you come back from the river, grab the machete because the grass in the patio is tall, I have to do everything, you see it all just like me but you don't see we have to clean it up, we can't live like animals in the middle of the bush, you have to be clean and neat no one is going to come to clean your house (in his African way of speaking, cleanliness is next to godliness), where you live all is dirty and messy, it's a sign that your souls are dirty, I don't want dirty children, not in body not in soul, God will ask me for an account of your acts, that's why he sent you to me, all I do is comply with his divine will, but what a burden, Lord, Lord how heavy, O Lord. We thought all this along with my father, because that's the mood he was always in.

But that day as I took off the sheet I was wearing as a chasuble and tried (unsuccessfully) to hide the signs of my secret game, he went calmly into his room, and he never mentioned the incident again. From that moment, I noticed he was paying attention to certain things: he relieved me of some chores so I could study, and when Father Ortiz came by, they would go off whispering to one another on the dusty road that went by our house. In the darkness, relieved only by the glow of a waning moon, I spied them from my hiding place behind the fence that separates our patio from the rest of the world right under the *atanga* tree; I could barely figure out what they were saying; the black man was invisible from where I was, and the white man had no head or hands, and all I could see was his long white tunic. I know he has a vocation, father, he is very devout and obedient; I'm sure the Lord has chosen him even though he hasn't told me, let's not lose him. I too have noticed he's different from the others, humble and alert, a blessing the Lord sends to your house. Praise be to God, father, God sends me children so I can guide them through the straight and narrow, and he always knows the reason for his holy will. Well, he should study diligently, the designs of God are inscrutable; you are a good and honorable man with a fear of God, perhaps it's his wish to bless your home with his infinite goodness by choosing your firstborn for this mission. Yes, father, like sending his firstborn to save us; how good it will be if this comes to be, father; may God hear you.

Weeks after my secret was discovered, they told me I was going to receive First Communion on the day of our patron, Saint James.

In those days it was not normal for a child of nine to receive First Communion, but they all agreed—Don Ramón, my father, Ambrosio the catechist—that I was virtuous enough, so Father Ortiz decided to give me Holy Comunion. Ambrosio the catechist's lessons every afternoon after rosary complemented Don Ramón's intensive preparations on Thursday mornings. Actually, none of that was a problem for me because I already knew the catechism by heart, including all the prayers, supplications, and ejaculatories.

One day, mother took me to Señor Casamitjana's trade station in the capital of the district. Casamitjana was the white man who bought all my father's coffee and cocoa; he often visited our house. Before he left, he used to give my brothers and me a ride through town in his "piku" —his pick-up truck. He would always address my father with a "don," and my father called him "señor" despite their friendship. They measured my legs, arms, and back, and between Doña Montserrat Montesinos Casamitjana—Señora M M to her friends—Policarpo (Casamitjana's trading-post clerk), and my mother, they calculated the number of meters of white fabric necessary to make my little sailor suit. On the way back, we went into the tailor's house where the bus stops; it was long in the front, and the cabin was made of wood like those trucks I see around here that transport dangerous animals. The seats were hard; I jumped over them only to sit down in the space between them. There were just a couple of windows; a little fresh air managed to get in along with Rio Muni's typical red dust. We had the privilege of sitting in old Reo's seat, next to the white driver, because my father is an emancipated black man, but that day the cabin was occupied by some white people, including a little boy, all going to Ebebiyin. It was the first time I had seen such a small white person. Seriously, he looked a little like Baby Jesus. After that day when I was coming home from church, I went over to the tailor's house to see if he had finished my sailor's suit for Communion. I observed how it was made, the tailor carefully cutting the fabric with a pair of big rusty scissors; a meter of the cloth had been stripped off, leaving holes showing the weft. That's how some of the dresses came out, especially the ones for fat women, the tailor's feet in rapid motion pedaling the old alpha sewing machine, the right one moving downward and the left upward. The floor of the shop was carpeted with fabric remnants and thread: red, blue, white—a butterfly cut right in the middle, and to one side a white clipping with black patches.

And in the final rehearsal, accompanied by my mother and her sisters Eulalia (we called her Eu) and Tecla (we called her Te), and my little granny Josefina, always and forever called Mama Fina. The tailor was putting the final touches on the suit, more for show than for efficiency, and how beautiful the long white pants looked on me, the first long pants in my life, and the white shirt with a blue sailor's collar on the back, and a bow, also blue, whose purpose was, I imagine, besides adornment, to hide the snap lock that made the neck look shorter. Emblazoned on the uniform was a blue braid embroidered at the lower sleeve in the form of a ship's handrail. I imagine my mother was remotely inspired by the suit worn by the governor general when he visited the continental area, or perhaps she was advised by Señora

M M, I don't know, because I had never seen the governor general and didn't know who he looked like, although he must have looked very elegant because everyone said so. They bought me a bright-colored rosary—just like the one Our Lady had given to the shepherds of Fatima, a friend of my father had commented—and a little Regina missal. It was very white with a mother-of-pearl cover, a little angel outlined in gold was painted on it, and a little metal lock like the one Padre Ortiz had. And that May I was more devout than ever. And like the other first communicants, I went to school in the morning and to church in the afternoon with flowers for the Virgin Mary, our mother. I made beautiful bouquets of begonia, tropical flowers, ylang-ylang, roses—red, yellow, white, pink—for my brothers and sisters and for me. And after the rosary vespers, we approached the altar with my father toward the front of the chapel, where in the left corner there was an icon of the Virgin that had been propped on a chair covered by a pure white sheet and lighted by two candles—or an oil lamp depending on who knows what. And at her feet we ceremoniously placed the flowers. The women and men wore their scapularies, rosaries in their hands, all in procession chanting Marist hymns. I distinguished the poor among us by their dusty, torn scapularies and their makeshift rosaries, which they put together with whatever they could find in the bush and which someone in town would tie together with a fine wire and a pair of small, finely pointed pliers for ten *pesetas*, I think. These rosaries had not been blessed, though they too had their little medals and crosses, because the only rosaries blessed by Padre Ortiz went for twenty-five. They were the ones with big black beads disdained by the most devout, who preferred the expensive ones.

Two days prior to the twenty-fifth of July, the feast of Saint James, patron saint of Spain and my town, Ambrosio the catechist tested us in front of Padre Ortiz. It was something of a confirmation because those of us present that afternoon had already gone through Don Ramón's arduous exams. Three or four of them flunked, as I recall, yes, three or four, because all of a sudden they had forgotten the Ten Commandments, or they got very nervous when they recited prayers to the Lord Jesus Christ, or they didn't remember what they had to do or say when they went to confession, or they didn't understand the long question Father Ortiz asked them—name-the-seven-virtues-and-the-seven-deadly-sins—and they were silent, although I think they flunked because they were not watching the catechist Ambrosio's lips, who was mouthing the words of the catechism, the first words of the correct answers behind Father Ortiz's back so that his students would get the right answers. The town looked magnificent, triumphal arches here and there, braided palm wreaths adorned with flowers, each with its own emblem—ducks, goats, chickens, and all kinds of things. Palm wine was abundant, and every afternoon before the feast of Saint James, I saw people getting off the bus with cases of cognac and dry gin. And the women spent the whole afternoon braiding each other's hair, and when they saw head lice they would scratch that spot and the one whose head was being scratched would calmly say, yes right there, sighing with pleasure and the other one would take it out with her finger nail and tear it apart with her teeth. Yes, everybody was happy and all dressed up, people would come from far-off towns just to attend the feast day of my town. After Mass there would be a big dinner with Father Ortiz presiding as well as the Colonial Police. And Ambrosio the catechist was at the same table with Father Ortiz and the police, as proud as a peacock, and Don Ramón was there with the chiefs of all the surrounding tribes, the freed slaves, and the most notable people of the district. And at the dining table there would be tuna in oil, black olives, and red wine. Later there would be a fair and evening celebrations. And the little girls joined hands and formed a perfect circle as they sang popular songs about the Basque country, showing their shiny white teeth, all the shinier as they blended with the white uniforms, their bleached *wambas*, socks covering their ankles, plain skirts amply fringed at the knee. They formed a perfect circle as they swirled and danced, showing, for a split second, their black thighs crowned by a white triangle, a tight white blouse that showed the incipient protuberances of their upper bodies or sometimes a consolidated roundness, a bracelet with rings of various colors, and finally a red scarf. In church, this was knotted under their chins, but for the festivities the scarves were tied around their necks, like the uniform of the Founder, allowing full view of their artistically braided hair. And then the children's three-legged race, or climbing a pole greased with palm oil with a little flag on top to see who could get up and down the fastest, and the winner was allowed to join the legendary heroes of the district—this was the strategy of modernity. And the soccer match, the last round of the tournament that had left two teams for the playoffs—the only lasting vestige of our past fratricidal wars converted today in a fraternity of sport by the magnificence of civilization. It was played in the dirt patio at school, with two rocks that marked each goal and the referee interrupting the game constantly to determine if the ball had gone over the imaginary out-of-bounds line; at times a goal would be nullified despite what Pio said, because he was lame. And children recited poetry honoring Saint James the Apostle or the Virgin or Father Claret. At dusk, in the final stage of the celebration, the emblem of the official festivities, the prizes—soccer balls, colored pencils, fountain pens, a copy of *Djoba, Nguema, Bokesa*, a watch—were awarded by Father Ortiz and the Colonial Police Lieutenant. And when the authorities crossed the bridge, leaving a cloud of dust in the horizon, the townspeople would be free to begin the real party and drink as they pleased, and the night would be filled with shouts, songs, dances, drums, and vomiting, and some were found sleeping it off in a ditch, having consumed too much *malamba* and gin.

Mama had washed, starched, and ironed my white sailor suit a few days before. My grandparents had come along with all my aunts and uncles from both sides of the families from far-off places, some even from the other side of the border, the ones I had not met until then. My father was very pleased and proud of his firstborn son, me of course. People in the district were saying this was the first time someone so young had received his First Communion. It was a historical event, and this is why the festivities would have to be more elaborate than usual; not to worry, he said to mommy one night. He would find a way to excuse himself from the notables so that he

74

could be at home with the invited guests from town. I had gone to confession with my fellow first communicants the day before; I don't know what sin I had committed. It was three in the afternoon, and after that point I would no longer be able to eat or drink anything until after Mass. I remember being the center of attention amid all the emotion, the hubbub of the preparation, the excitement of donning my little suit with long pants, having to put up with the slaps on my back—they thought they were pats. And in the middle of the night—or was it early morning?—I woke up terribly hungry. I prayed for the hunger to go away, but it was intense, however hard I tried not to think about it, and the whole house smelled like roasted goat, duck, rice and tomato sauce, yams, and tapioca, and the aroma made its way into my nostrils and almost down to my stomach. Saliva was dribbling from my mouth, and my stomach lining seemed to stretch as far as my backbone, and I held on to my midsection to avoid a disaster, my head was spinning.

It was the temptation of the devil, the supreme test I had been waiting for that would put my faith on trial. I put myself in the hands of my godfather, Mary Ever Virgin, and my dear Guardian Angel, in you I trust, while it occurred to me that this was all a dream. And I fully woke up in the kitchen with my mouth filled with lamb meat, licking my ten greasy fingers, and then I realized that I had just devoured some chicken in peanut sauce, rice in tomato sauce, duck, just about everything I had found in the kitchen. Everyone was asleep. The devil made me do it, I thought; I was horrified, it was he who guided my hands through the darkness to find my way to the enormous kitchen. And now I was terribly thirsty, but you can't drink water either, it's a sin and you know it, but I've got meat and a banana that want to pass through my throat, and I can barely breathe, so I drank some water and felt much better. I went back to bed; that night my two little brothers were in the same bed with me. Confession was no longer an option because I had already done it, even though father was sleeping just two rooms away form mine; in any case confession would be to no avail, because I had to fast for twenty-four hours. I couldn't receive Communion the next day. I spent the rest of the night restless, listening to my father snoring—those loud, gruff snores were my father's, the whistling ones were Auntie Asilda's—my brother wouldn't stop fidgeting, he had his feet on my full belly, I shoved them off, and that's how I spent the rest of the night, so earnestly sorry for my sin. And I promised to tell my father what I did, and that I could not receive Holy Communion in a state of mortal sin.

When my Tía Tecla, the one we called Te, came in to get me up, I was already awake. She bathed me very carefully even though I had always washed on my own, and I suppose she did not observe that my stomach was swollen because she put brilliantine all over me, and when I placed each leg into the pants she was holding for me, I didn't feel anything, and she told me my outfit would be the prettiest one. Terrified, I asked myself if they would find the mess in the kitchen, but everyone was rushing around and I could not even talk to my father. The first *tumba* call to Mass, hurry up, my father said, and everyone scurrying around: Where did you put the comb? Who was the last one to use the soap? Let's see, you clean that boy, why does he have to get dirty now? And all that was going on around me without my realizing it; I was thinking about my sin, and I suppose everyone thought I was so thoughtful and repentant because I was thinking about receiving the body of Christ. Then the second call to Mass, surely it was my cousin Paco, he had his own drum style. We left the house; I was between my mother and father; he was wearing a dark suit and she a shawl with the mother-of-pearl regina missal, and the rosary with multicolored beads was in my hands. Slowly, devoutly, we proceeded, but I felt I was the devil himself, the sinner; how could you fall into temptation, you can't confess again, how can I tell him now that we're almost at the chapel, beg the priest for another confession, he's still in the confessional, what a shame to have to go to confession again in front of everyone, they would let me receive Holy Communion and everybody will know about it, better to just keep on going, I'll confess after Communion.

It was getting hotter, being close to midday, and there was no room left in the church. The first communicants were in the low benches, the boys on the left of the altar and the girls on the right; the men also were on the left and the women on the right side of the chapel—mixing was forbidden, it was sinful. I was in the first of three rows of communicants, and everyone could see me and I could see everyone. My father was toward the back, in praying position.

The Mass began, Gregorian chant since it was a special day; then came Father Ortiz's long sermon against the heathens, reminding us how Saint James's steed had helped win the battle against them. And I gazed at the saint's unsheathed sword with the sharp tip pointing upwards, the muscular hindquarters of the pure white horse with its straight tail, its rear right hoof sunk into the eye of a heathen who was pleading for his life, hands in the air and wearing an expression of sheer pain, and its left leg resting on the midsection of another heathen, whose turban was falling off. And between the horse's legs, the grisly figure of yet another one, his black face filled with terror, about to receive the mortal blow of our patron saint in all his justice, and I had such a stomachache that I began to sweat profusely. When it stopped, Ambrosio the catechist was eagerly translating the sermon, and since he could not remember the whole of Father Ortiz's hour-long homily, he made up a few ideas to make sure his time equaled that of the priest. He always does that, perhaps because Father Ortiz has no idea what he's saying and the parishioners have no idea what he has said either. The heat was stultifying, and the humidity made it worse, and Ambrosio was taking too long—had we been in the church for three and a half hours?—and the mortal sin moved right into my belly, giving me gas, so I had to put pressure on my anal muscles not to let it out. And that physical torment was nothing but the manifestation of the spiritual torment I was feeling, you can't receive Communion like this, but I can't do anything about it now, I'll confess the next time Father Ortiz comes by, and Ambrosio was turning toward us at that moment, just as Father Ortiz had done when he spoke of the purity of our souls, a purity we must maintain. Our mothers and fathers would be responsible before God if we shunned the immaculate whiteness symbolized by the clothes we were wearing, even though Ambrosio was saying something completely different. I was jolted by the sound of hundreds of bodies standing up at the same time, and the boy beside me gave me a nudge and I was alert for a short time; oh God, on top of it all, I'm falling asleep in Mass the very day of my First Communion, and I tried to see if my father had noticed. Fortunately there were too many people between our bench and his pew, and there was a tree trunk used as a column between us.

As the girls were approaching the priest to receive Communion, I was sweating and trembling in fear, how can you receive the Lord in a state of mortal sin? You will never be forgiven, you'll be condemned to hell, but if I don't go up to receive Communion, everyone will notice, and my father will beat me to death, and now I was sweating even more, and from so much squeezing my buttocks, now I had to pee, stay strong, the last girl has just received the Host, just keep it in. When the priest turned to us and the first boy went forward, I was sure I'd be struck by the Lord's lightning, look at you, the sacrilege you have committed against the Body of Christ the very first day, and I kept my thighs as close together as possible putting as much pressure as I could on them, like that; but it hurt down there, and I was sweating even more because it was impossible to do it all: stand up, walk toward the priest, kneel down, stick out my tongue, say amen, close my mouth without biting the priest's fingers like some old ladies did, and then get up again and go back to my seat slowly and devoutly. As I was about to get back to my empty seat, the floodgate opened and out came the stream. The same way as in dreams, I sensed the warmth in my underpants, then in my pants down into my thighs, knees, legs, socks, all the way to my white shoes, and the water made a trail to my place. This is God's punishment for having received Him in a state of mortal sin; God punishes without the rod! was what my father was shouting inside of me, and I felt deep shame accompanied by a conviction that the Christ I had on my tongue had decided not to enter me: I couldn't swallow, my mouth was completely dry. The church was full, I felt all eyes on me, as well as the unbearable heat, so hot it felt cold on my body. And at the very instant I knelt down, facing the crowd again from the same seat I had had before, I felt an emptiness in my lower stomach and hollowness in my head; instinctively I shut my eyes, but it was impossible to prevent it: I was about to throw up and I tried not to by swallowing the vomit so that nobody would see. I felt the warmth and smelled the odor at the same time, and my little sailor suit was turning dark red, the stain of sin, the color of the meat and peanut sauce I had eaten the night before and hadn't digested. I fell down, and my last semiconscious sensation was dominated by an intense dread: fear is cold; I saw myself in hell for ever and ever for not having obeyed the Law of God, fasting and abstaining from meat, this is what the Holy Mother the Church calls for. The Church stipulated twenty-four hours before Communion. I had died in mortal sin.

For months I didn't want to see anybody, no one at all, not my brothers and sisters, my friends, or my schoolmates. In every face I saw their smirks, and they laughed for good reason: I had peed in my pants, in church no less, and I vomited the Sacred Communion Wafer. I became a recluse, and I never wore my sailor suit again or any

of the accessories. And every time I saw a friend in white communion clothes, I felt ridiculous, nauseated, and the stink and warmth
of the vomit came back to me. My father avoided me for a long time,
and when we were together I felt he wanted to tell me something,
or do something, but his own silence made him less daunting than
he might have been, and fortunately my mother was always close by,
calling him, and I suppose she placated him. This incident was never
spoken of in my presence, but I still felt shame inside me, and I knew
I had hurt my father deeply, I had disappointed him, I made him the
laughingstock of the whole world. From that moment I no longer pretended to say Mass in my room. I nearly gave up praying. I no longer
thought about becoming a priest, I didn't want anything at all: no
matter what I did, I would carry the stigma with me forever, and I
would never again be worthy as a firstborn son. And a few years later
I came across the rosary with multicolored beads and the little *Regina Missal* with designs on the cover, slightly stained by something
like a brown polish; it was in a closet drawer my father kept for things
he couldn't throw away.

four

Tío Abeso wanted you to be as good a hunter as he was, and he often brought you into the forest to inspect his traps. Sometimes you'd find a trapped genet, an antelope, or a porcupine. He called you when he was about to go hunting with his rifle; he killed toucans, boars, even elephants and crocodiles. You saw him take aim, concentrate, hold his breath, and you'd take cover behind a tree. When the shot fired, you would only come out after the smoke had stopped pouring out of both barrels, and the forest would be filled with the smell of gunpowder. Then you ran over to the fallen squirrel and poked it with your stick, or you waited until your uncle shot the wild boar. You walked all day following the gigantic footprints of a herd of elephants, or you would detect a rabbit that looked like a cloud with its white spot on its back, or my uncle would suddenly tense up and stop you, listening intently to a noise, which would gradually get louder, and just at that moment you spotted the horned snake spying our every move. But none of this made you tired or scared because these outings were fun, and because your uncle reassured you all was safe. Abeso was older than your father; he was the purveyor of your tradition, the natural chief of our tribe and our lineage. He told you about how Motulu Mbenga, your great-grandfather, had arrived at the place all of you live now, had founded your village and placed it under the protection of the totemic animal, the alligator; an alligator had helped your father's grandfather cross the Ntem River; he had been defeated by the French conquerors many years ago and had to flee south. The alligator was one of the tribe's taboos, the most important one; he protected the chiefs and elders of your lineage, children and pregnant women also; he sheltered you from scheming demons and enemy spirits; he was the steadfast protector of what was yours, no matter how intangible, land both private and communal, belonging to all the descendants of Motulu Mbenga. The alligator should be respected, it must not be touched, and any one of the descendants of Motulu Mbenga who harmed or killed an alligator, even by accident, must be condemned. And you asked silly questions, what if the alligator attacks you? And Tío Abeso assured you that no alligator attacked a descendant of Motulu Mbenga; an occurrence like that was a forecast of bad times for the clan. Then he told you about the times before the arrival of the white occupiers, when there had been many cases of alligators attacking human beings.

You would return home with the last rays of light through the narrow path that thousands of bare feet had patiently shaped in the bush; your uncle talked as he walked behind you, carrying two large monkeys whose blood was still flowing over their torsos. And you held your father's empty rifle with extreme caution—your uncle couldn't get a license according to the white man's laws—and he walked along, talking about how in the old days the alligators had gone crazy. They came out of the streams and onto the trails to attack humans, women, and children, and the prophecy had come true: a detachment of foreign troops had occupied the region, and our spears and poisoned arrows were worth nothing because the foreigners had firearms, many of them, like the one you were carrying on your shoulder. And they had brought gifts for the weak chiefs who signed a peace treaty without doing battle; the gifts were worth nothing—useless, colored *clotes*, bits of broken mirrors—and they made them drunk with that liquid that burned the throat; listen my son, those weak chiefs signed peace treaties without having fought, this is why ambition is very bad, it's the worse sickness that a man can have. And your tribe lost strength because the white man's weapons exterminated the alligators.

Those stories fascinated you—the only one who tried to preserve the collective memory of your people was Tío Abeso. His mission was to revive the essence of your caste, to shape your young and still tender spirit with what remained of your fallen culture. He saw no advantage at all in making friends with the white occupiers; he preferred keeping intact the magical powers, mysterious and dangerous, powers that had been bestowed to him as chief. And that was the origin of his contempt of those who were ignorant of your people, a contempt you thought was spite. At that time there were many things you didn't understand, and you were rather skeptical too because you had heard your father say that no black man had invented anything, not even a pin. What can anyone expect from a civilization incapable of inventing, people who worshiped fetishes, people who had been defeated by the carriers of the One Truth? Then your uncle answered by telling you a story, another type of legend, like the one about the tortoise and the tiger fighting each other over control of the animal kingdom, one with astuteness, the other with fear and contempt for others. They were moral tales where astuteness and patience always won over pride and brutality, and the tortoise always ended up tricking and ridiculing the tiger. Tío Abeso was saying that infinite patience and constant cleverness of your tribe, your caste, your people, would always triumph in the end over the ostentation and arrogance of the occupiers. But you were incapable then of interpreting the parables around you. Instead, you were taken in by other allegories, impressed by the power that you saw in those who brought the One True Faith. You were too conceited to value the age-old wisdom contained in the legends, stories, prophecies, and myths that seemed so simple; you were too much a child to understand that your existence would be justified only in these words.

I liked to be in my uncle's cabin. He shunned the dwellings that imitated the style of the whites; his house was some distance apart from the main village at the edge of the forest, because he didn't like the road and had opposed its construction. His little house was made of tree trunks he had tied together with *melongo* fibers; it had a grass roof supported by bamboo rafters, and between them he had spread adobe made from mud he himself had mixed by stamping on it with his own feet. There were two small rooms and a spacious one. Around it were six dwellings, forming a semicircle, with ducks and chickens in front; these were the six abodes of his six wives and their children. Some of the children were grown and married and lived in the village on the road. Others were my age. I really liked it when Father Ortiz came; he used to stay at our house, and we would go over to Tío Abeso's place. Father Ortiz was determined to convert Tío Abeso; it was his apostolic mission. He wanted him to give up five of his wives and marry his first by the Church; she was the only one the priest considered legitimate. He called the other ones concubines. I was the translator as he spoke of the One True Religion, the death and resurrection of Christ for the redemption of mankind, and my uncle looked at him with the disdainful expression he reserved for white people. He asked the priest if he had ever seen all he was describing, and the priest said no, that it was a tradition, so then Tío Abeso said that he too could tell the priest about the traditions of his tribe because all tribes have their own traditions, and the secret of living in peace was for all the tribes to practice their own traditions without interfering with the others or trying to influence the powers of the amulets that protected another tribe. All traditions have things that are true and things that are false or at least exaggerated, and no single one of them could be considered the one true religion. My uncle would say this as he brushed away flies with a small broom—he had nerves of steel. The priest would become uncontrollably angry: How dare you compare the Revealed Truth with your fetishes and your idol worship! He would call my uncle a blasphemer and tell him he would go to hell. And with infinite patience Tío Abeso answered that at that moment they were not in the territory of the white man's tribe, that *he* hadn't gone to the other man's tribe trying to convert everyone to his belief, and he told the priest that there was no reason for him to be angry, and he asked him whether he could give me any idea how to find that place where I will burn, and whether he has been there. The priest admitted that he had never seen hell, but that the revealed doctrine, the dogma of the One True Church, and all biblical tradition testified to the existence of hell, the place reserved for the souls of dead sinners, and the worst sin of all was to deny the presence of the One God and the Trinity. Tío then asked if the dead of the white man's tribe ever came back to tell what they had seen beyond the great river, and the priest asked how could that be, and that my uncle was making fun of him because he should know that in no part of the world do dead people come back to life. And my uncle answered, so how do you know what happens to a man after he dies? And the priest's best answer was faith: faith in God, in his revealed doctrine, in the Church founded by his Only Son. And Tío said that he too had faith in his tradition, much faith, and just as the priest would never agree to convert to his creed because he didn't understand anything about it, so it was useless to hope that my uncle would ever be baptized. And with his eyes lost in the dusk, he asked if it was possible to trust the honor of a man who emptied out his most intimate feelings for a bunch of unproved words or for being able to eat olive oil. The priest then scolded him for having so many women, and my uncle said that he had heard that the white man's god had told his people to be fruitful and multiply so that they would not disappear from the face of the earth because he had made them in his own image. Father Ortiz nodded, seemingly satisfied. And Tío asked the priest if he too abided by God's mandate to be fruitful. The priest was exasperated, and grew quite angry, and tried to explain how he was serving God by sacrificing and living a chaste life by renouncing the flesh, how God loves the pure and not the licentious, those who spend all their lives fornicating, day and night, just for fleshly pleasure. Tell me, would you be telling me all this now if your mother and father were like you? I translated the question, and the priest was silent, his face red with rage. And my uncle then said that he couldn't believe in him because he himself had heard the priest say that his god created the world and had given man superior intelligence so that he could use it, and the priest was the first one not to abide by the mandate given by his own god. Tell him I can't understand how God can tell everyone to multiply and then say he prefers the ones who don't, the ones who go through this life without sowing a single seed. Or is it that whites have a special magic that allows them to propagate without touching a woman? Then the priest began to talk very fast in a language that was not Spanish, looking dejected, monotonously repeating a single short word that I couldn't translate into Fang because I didn't know what he was saying either. And Tío Abeso called his fist wife, Mama Andeme, and told her to take the duck with the black and white feathers and give it to the priest as a sign of their hospitality. You are both our guest and our neighbor, he told me to translate, and although we don't agree on anything, I must give you this duck to show we are good neighbors. Neighbors must always understand each other above and beyond their ideas, just as one of our proverbs says: hunger will pass, but its legend will stay. The gesture seemed to placate Father Ortiz, who accepted the duck, and he took out a case from the sack he was carrying and a pack of cigarettes of strong tobacco, which my uncle started to chew, and later had some of it ground up so that he could sniff it. I'll baptize you one of these days, my stubborn old friend, and I translated this for my uncle, because I am here to convert all of you to the One True Faith. And my uncle said that he already had a name, the one that his father had given him at birth, and no god of any other tribe could be offended by the fact that his name was his name, and he reminded the priest of his very own words, that all men are children of God. But to be a child of God, one first had to be baptized to enter into his sacred temple. And my uncle replied that birth comes before the name, and that you can't give a man a new name when he has had one for such a long time. I have twenty-eight children—tell him—and don't love one more than another, and each one has a name and his own temperament. Why does his God have to punish me for calling myself what my people have called me forever? Go ahead, tell him. The priest responded by saying that Christian names have symbolic meaning, so that the baptized can follow the model of virtue manifested by the devoted saint who has the same name. Then my uncle rose up from his little bamboo bed, fixed his eyes on Father Ortiz, and calmly and with infinite patience explained through me that his name as well as the names of his twenty-eight children were all endowed with symbolic meaning. Abeso had been the last chief of our tribe, and if he carried that name, it was because the elders had elected him as successor, and from childhood he had been entrusted to the chief so that he could learn patience from him, justice, and the necessary conviction to be a worthy heir. And he had faithfully carried out his charge until the new white masters who had come from the other side of the world changed the customs of our people. And with his lofty manner, suddenly invested with a mysterious and magical dignity, looking squarely into the eyes of Father Ortiz as if he could understand him, Tío Abeso asked him to explain if there was any difference between the meaning of his name and the new name the priest wanted to impose on him. I knew all about the virtues of Chief Abeso Motulu, he said; I learned from him to love my people, I was granted our sacred tradition by him, when he died he handed over to me the amulets with which our tribe has defended itself from our enemies for many years, gems that I must pass on to my successor. I fought at his side on the day of his death; as a warrior he was fierce like a lion, smart as a leopard, prudent and wise as a tortoise, generous as an alligator, soft as a cat, stubborn as an old rooster, happy as a monkey, agile as an antelope. What do I know of your Saint James? I've heard people talk about his feats, but I've never seen them, and they are said to have occurred on the other side of the earth, and they didn't affect the life of our tribe. I want to be called Abeso so that everybody knows me and remembers me as such; that name identifies me, it gives me life, it's what allows me to be who I am and not someone else. The priest listened intently, and now he chose his words carefully. You should be a model—and he patted my uncle on the knee a few times—because you are the head of the tribe, and you should understand that times have changed. The world advances, and it's important for your tribe to leave its primitive ways behind. We've brought civilization, we cure your sickness, we've brought peace, and we've fought your barbarity. And don't deny that eating human flesh and worshiping alligators are barbaric customs. Now as I translated his words, he was laughing smugly, intently watching Tío's reaction: his wrinkled tattooed face, his white head. Surely you won't deny that eating your fellow beings, your brothers, is an ugly custom…My uncle didn't let me finish the sentence and replied: the only ones who ate human flesh were sorcerers, and not everyone was a sorcerer. It was not in the least barbaric to venerate the alligator, a creature that had been of great service to our tribe, because he himself wouldn't be sitting here now if it weren't for an alligator. Don't you pamper and respect the illustrious members of your people, those you call saints? Isn't that sculpture on the chapel the figure of an animal? I see the images on your temples and I assume they are nothing but totems, the remains of your glorious ancestors. I don't know your language, but at times I hear the catechist read from the book of your tradition that the one you call Jesus was killed by the people of his tribe for being good. And you eat his flesh and drink his blood because you believe this will make you good. You worship him in all his forms, when he was a child, when he had a beard; and after he died, you parade his cadaver around on the days you lament his death. Isn't this just what we do? If I keep Abeso Motulu's skeleton in my house, it's because it makes me feel safe and gives me strength, and it encourages me to follow his example. You never knew your king, but you don't stop following him, you keep his example. I knew Abeso Motulu well, and this is why his head continues to guide my acts and the acts of my tribe. You are the sorcerer of your tribe, and that's why you eat the flesh and drink the blood of your god. What's wrong with our doing the same with our venerated figures? The head of a wise man should serve as an example for our young, so that when we speak of him, it won't be an empty legend. And we must tell them that here is the man who did this and that for us, for the people, for our tribe or the clan, and it's up to you to follow his example. We don't read books. We know our tradition because the eldest member passes it on to the young so that when he too is old, he will in turn impart the tradition to his young. This is how we have always lived. You say you have brought medicine, but you found medicine here too. You say you have brought peace, but you were the ones who incited war. And tell me, don't the tribes of white people fight among themselves? The only problem I see with you is that you want us to give up our customs and trust your ancestors. And that can't be. I can't tell the member of another tribe to honor the figure of Motulu Mbenga, because it means nothing to him. The priest kept looking at me; surely he thought he should not have brought me because I should not have heard such things, but he couldn't have communicated with my uncle if I hadn't been there. I was indispensable, a necessary device to accomplish his apostolic mission. And the priest then started praising the example of my baptized father, who had married through the Church without concubines or illegitimate children. These were virtues that God would compensate, since he had gained full emancipation, a condition allowing him to enjoy advantages out of the reach of stubborn heathens. And my uncle looked at him with a hint of anger, only I could detect it, and he looked at me with a trace of sadness that rubbed off on me, and he said that the god of the white people was a very simple god who only saw what was good for the whites. He added that he didn't want to argue with the priest about matters only relevant to his family, because it was not good that family quarrels be aired in the company of guests. Family relations are like a nightingale caught in a trap: even as it rots, it will always be hanging by a vein. And in the fading light of an oil lamp recently cleaned and lit by my cousin Micue, the third child of Tío Abeso's fourth wife, a conversation that never went anywhere was languishing; lots of talk, no substance, declared my uncle, but this filled me with desolation. Here I was in the middle of a conflict, and I couldn't take sides; I was observing the last splendors of a world that was disappearing forever, and another very different one was arriving; I couldn't embrace either one. Now I know that the priest, who simply called my uncle Friend, knew very well he was in the presence of an exceptional man, a man with whom he must do battle, because my uncle accepted his cases of cognac to avoid a disagreement even though he didn't drink those types of libations since for Abeso they were symbols of the oppressors' domination. Just one time I heard what might be considered praise for Father Ortiz from my uncle: if it weren't for the way they all want everyone to be like them, he'd be quite acceptable. But right away he added: I suppose, though, if it weren't for that, they never would have found their way here.

five

"See you February fifteenth, God willing!"

"Have a wonderful time!"

It was a fifteenth of December, and all the kids were running toward the dusty road, their white uniforms a little more wrinkled, the *Second Grade Notebooks*—or was it the *Dalmau Carles Pla Encyclopedia*—tucked under their sweaty underarms, a few pages fluttering in the warm breeze between the trees in the village. I wasn't running. I would have preferred to stay at school that year, not have to be the focus of my father's stern gaze: now that you're here, son, you must go to work harvesting cocoa beans, work is most important, no one should sit around all day doing nothing, you're a man now, and you must help me, this is why you have to go to the plantation, take off what you're wearing and put on your work clothes. It was hot and humid in the middle of the day, and I took off my white shirt, white pants, and white moccasins and put on work clothes that made me look like a raggedy little day laborer, early signs of industriousness that my father insisted on instilling in his only son, a category he demoted to firstborn. He grabbed the machete firmly; from time to time he would use it to cut a weed growing in the path leading into the bush. The animals fled from the presence of my father as he murmured a monotonous litany of proverbs and sayings; I trailed behind, walking along without listening, my mind in a blank, unsuccessfully trying to figure out the direction of the clouds, red, gray, blue, superimposed right there at the opening of the forest. In the midst of all the lush vegetation there was a dark patch, purple and yellow leaves crackled at our feet. And I saw Don Ramón again, a row of white teeth protruding from his dark gums, holding his punishing *melongo* whip transformed into a baton, which he waved as he led the last chorus of children in a procession that had formed at the entrance of the school with its grass roof and stained white *calabo* walls.

I planted all this myself, my father would say proudly yet humbly, pointing to his cocoa and coffee groves, a harmonious mixture of both. All I want is for you to be worthy and to carry on the work I've begun. I hope you're not going to be like those sons in that parable, who spent their inheritance frivolously.

And I thought that none of that was any good; I refused to imagine my life going on and on, day after day, always, back and forth between the coffee and cocoa groves and the brick house built of cement and zinc, machete on my shoulder, my old khaki pith helmet on my shaved head, my colored shirt, all tattered. I looked like a time-worn black explorer, mosquitoes biting my bare arms, sweaty, smelly, half starved, unable to eat, a slave forever in a deal made with Don Santos Casamitjana, the white man who bought our coffee and cocoa and in return provided us with rice, salted fish, fabric, cans of preserves, but no money. He would make this payment when we delivered many sacks of coffee and cocoa. But I also asked myself if my desire to get out of there was proof my father was right, that I just didn't like to work. It was comforting to convince myself I did like to work but just didn't like that kind of work; yet there was a lingering doubt. And I encouraged myself by repeating that I was not a good-for-nothing lazy little black boy, so I kept on with the machete, chopping the stalk of the pineapple without wounding its trunk or branch, spine bent to pick every yellow-ripe piece of fruit one by one, stoically putting up with it all. What choice did I have until I could escape with some excuse or other, but what excuse—the insect bites and the bees buzzing around the fruit? I heroically lifted the heavy straw basket filled to the brim, using the little strength I had in my young back, a sticky liquid dripping from the basket into my sweat. I was tired even before I started; I emptied the basket into the cocoa beans in a pile that spread out without getting too high—my father wanted it that way so he could be proud of how much he had worked. And that bluish sulfate, bitter and toxic, drenching the stems and leaves, the fruit, and my hands: be careful not to rub your eyes; impossible not to do that, father, I thought, don't you see the sweat dripping into my eyes? And the constant burning in my eyes, a snail's tentacles sunk into its own body, I pinched the soft flesh and it coiled back into its shell; I turned it over on the dark and tender earth and gazed at the thick foam; I grabbed the machete and pierced a hole in the snail's shell, and hung it by a piece of vine on a branch over the pile of cocoa beans. I was glad to have "hunted" such a large snail, and at that point my father told me I had earned myself a dinner. Women hunched over in their dirty wet rags passed by with their *melongo* baskets filled with yucca, yams, manioc, and tender corn, or with sugarcane, *bambucha*, or tender dates: just a glimpse of them made me a little hungry at first, famished later. And my father kept on singing as if it were nothing, an endless hymn, as he gathered what he could from the highest branches with a sharp, double-edged saw that looked like a parrot's beak. And finally we covered all those piles of pineapple with leaves and branches, ants crawling over the fruit, let's not make it easy for them; and then the comments from the adjoining coffee groves; this new grunt works a lot, see, in just one morning he's filled three sacks; his eyes were filled with greed; you must learn to work the land, you must devise new methods to increase production. Like him I wanted to put my hand in the sacks and caress the coffee beans, and what I got was a huge black centipede that automatically curled up on my index finger, making me feel sick to my stomach; what bad luck, I'll have to wash that centipede-stained finger for a whole week, and I won't be able to eat with it.

No. I didn't like that work, but what could I do? I lost confidence in my father and in all those who could have helped me escape from that land. My future was tied more than ever to the plantation, to that narrow path into the bush filled with hungry ants and coiled centipedes on my finger, all for handing over the sacks of coffee and cocoa beans earmarked for Don Santos Casamitjana in exchange for kilos of salted fish, rice, and cans of sardines in olive oil; I didn't like them as much as I had before. A machete struck clean, quick, strong, and furious, but the lizard ran away fast, taking cover under a rotting tree trunk surrounded by a cluster of young ferns. I didn't feel a thing, really, at first I only saw how the blood was flowing from my right big toe, the tip of the machete was red, but it was not the lizard's blood, no, the little stream was coming from my body, flowing into the spongy tender earth, and the sliced piece of flesh was still moving down into the sack of Don Santos Casamitjana's coffee beans.

My toe healed slowly, and it kept me from enjoying a real vacation. And now that I think of it, maybe my father was right when he said all too honestly that I was capable of cutting off my own toe so that I could spend my vacation in bed without having to work in the plantation. Tía Te had to come over to take care of us. The days are long in Equatorial Guinea when the adults leave the house to do their chores after morning prayers and a frugal breakfast—leftovers from the night before, until they return home after the sun has fallen behind the tallest trees. Tía Te used to take us to the river when she washed clothes or the dishes, or to give my brothers and sisters a bath, or bring water, and she always took the opportunity to dive into a pond that the men had created years ago by damming up a section of the river. Alone on the riverbank I would stare at her, her long neck, so flexible and round, and the little clumps of soapsuds that settled on her breasts. With her hand she would carefully push off some suds and separate a multicolored bubble and blow it gently into the air and watch as it broke when it landed on a leaf. Her long arms were speckled with foam, her hand gliding down her body, steadily along her back and thighs, then quickly up to her navel, three precise moves and into the waist-deep water. Small concentric circles traced her breasts on the clear surface of the water, and she stayed there, her legs straddled, rubbing her lower abdomen under the water with a trembling hand. Then she dipped in all the way except for her head, splashed around, picked up a stone, and threw it at the frogs croaking in the marshes. I barely saw the reflection of the sun on her tight, shiny, ebony buttocks, and the white arches of her feet pointing toward me. And that image was with me later, all the time, the entire afternoon and night, and I dreamed of her until her picture reappeared the following day, but I couldn't go into the water to relieve the heat I was feeling, I had to watch her from the riverbank because of my bandaged foot. Then I touched myself, I was hard, it was my earliest premonition of sin—who am I, after all, to triumph over temptation where Adam had failed, I assured myself—I could feel the taut little hairs like Beelzebub's horns. And when we walked back to the fenced property, Aunt Te carrying the metal washbowl and bucket on her braided head, with me leaning on her because of my bad foot—it hurt too much when I walked on the hard ground—I felt her firm breasts under her robe bouncing on my cropped head. Then, as she cradled my little brother to sleep or as she swept the kitchen, I inclined my head toward her because I didn't want to loose the sensation of her rhythmic swaying as she hummed a tune in her smooth, nasal voice.

I followed her around everywhere during those short, sweet Christmas seasons—it's strange that I still feel the fire today—spying her every move, especially when I saw her coming toward the banana grove at the back of our property, the farthest spot from the house in the patio; I crouched behind a tree, it was the closest I could get without being seen, a precision worthy of the Prince of Darkness. I stared at her, lost in myself, perspiring and shaking. And like a majestic ship, slow and beautiful, her image appeared to me when she leaned forward, spread her legs, lifted up her dress, and urinated, facing away from me. A drake was going after a duck that was waddling around in the banana grove; the duck fanned her feathers, exposing a pink circle, it was shiny, and a liquid secreted ever so slowly from the roundness. Between the legs of the drake, a curly and fleshy-white tissue was getting longer as the lady duck approached. She stopped abruptly, she let herself down on the ground and the drake mounted her, cackling in a frenzy, and when he finally let go, I went over to the duck without knowing exactly why, and felt the warmth of her insides, eagerly imitating the drake's desire. The duck fluttered, and just as I satisfied myself, her wings grew limp and she could barely walk. She remained in that position, very still; I fled to my house and shut myself in my room, crying, angry at the discovery of the pleasures of evil; more than anything I was upset that I couldn't tell anybody.

"You have pubic hair already. You're a man now."

Tía Te said this as she stroked her soapy hand over your groin gently, and she looked at you lovingly, the way she always looked at you. And you didn't answer; you were surprised, bewildered by the proximity of her naked breast—your head resting on her moving ribs, not daring to look at the drops descending from her navel and fading into the mysterious twisted tangle below.

"My, how you've grown lately."

She was saying this and sprinkling water over your buttocks from her cupped hands. The frogs were croaking on the riverbanks, but you didn't dare bend down to grab that stone gleaming at the bottom and throw it at them, or at her, but you observed how nature deceived you at a time you needed it most. Shamed by the horrendous happenings with the lady duck in the banana grove, you grabbed your clothes and ran off without drying yourself. Still running, you pulled on your clothes; you could hear her clear, warm laughter, she begged you to stay: don't be a brat, help with these plates, I have to carry the water bucket. You didn't stop until you got to the protective grating of the entrance, where you could look back to get a glimpse of her without really seeing her. You went to your room, buried your face in the bed, and began to cry, a whole life crying in bed, defenseless against everything and everybody, your feet kicking the wooden bed frame as you always did. The wound opened again, but you didn't feel the pain in your toe because the pain in your soul was a thousand times worse. You begged God to forgive all your sins, to take her out of your path; you wanted your path clean and beautiful, but now you were praying without your heart in it, without faith, without hope, just praying for the sake of praying, for consolation, to protect you from the edge of the cliff, flames under your feet, the devil holding on to your short pants and demons laughing mercilessly as they tugged at them, bringing them down, toward the eternal flame of hell. And your early career as an unforgivable sinner was well under way; it had been initiated three years earlier on the day of your First Communion—Father Ortiz had authorized it, after all, because no one had found the Sacred Host in the vomit, so it was assumed that you had swallowed it. And you went around looking haggard, that's the honest truth, alone and melancholy, a prophet tired of everything and everybody at such a young age, a feeble soul without direction or consolation, with no faith in yourself or in anybody or in anything, without hopes or aspirations, crushed beneath the weight of your sins. You went to confession but you lied to the priest, how can I tell him about the duck? He'll throw me out of the confessional instantly, and things will get even worse. And you added even more weight to the burden of your conscience; it was showing through your chronic weakness, the aimless way you walked, your disconsolate manner. And the endless nights without sleep, crying in bed, my dear boy, what's the matter? nothing mother; something's wrong, you must have tapeworm again; it's not that mom; well, be quiet because when your father comes home he'll beat it out of you, I'm very worried about you. You look like a soul in agony, look what an example you're setting for your little brothers and sisters, always breaking plates, always the same, you look very bad, go to bed without supper, out of my sight. And the concupiscent union with the lady duck, an explosion of repressed vitality and desire, the search for a broad new horizon: it all turned into greater remorse, melancholy, loneliness, disgust, youthful sensations that you alone learned to identify, emotions sublimated by ghostly soliloquies, a bitter purgative drunk to the dregs without a hand to caress your spirit and temper the tribulations of puberty. If only I had extended that saving hand to my soul and not to my flesh, it would have mitigated my loneliness; if only it had been She and not she.

You didn't hear her open the door. You had fallen asleep, you were panting convulsively, she stroked your face spotted by the beginnings of a cold sweat. She called you softly, and when you came back to the reality of that warm afternoon, filled with cries and waters, your head was in her lap, your hairless head resting on the silken smoothness of her pubis.

"Touch me here," she told you, and you touched her with the eagerness of a beginner, with repressed fear and nervousness; four years older than you, she was your aunt, she was your blood, from the same womb as your mother, and you touched her there, reaching down without thinking, without believing, without hoping, seeing her as a woman when she was actually just a little thing, and she seeing you as a man when in reality you were nothing, nothing but a little skeleton, a tormented kid, all skin and bones.

"That's how you do it."

She pulled you toward her as she sat in bed facing you. You

promised not to tell anyone; I won't tell anyone even if they hit me, your first amorous encounter; the heat was contagious and her freshness drew you to her, imperatively yet imperceptibly, until an awkward coupling. It was at the same hour as your daily solitary celebrations of Mass last year, in that very room, next to the table you pretended was an altar, sitting on the bed you pretended was a pulpit, on the sheet you pretended was a chasuble; but the icons on the wall had disappeared along with the evocation of the godfather sanctified by his purity. A solitary crucifix without Christ, deprived of all his collective strength, presided over the defiled room you pretended was a chapel. And the affliction hovering over the tribe, a great affliction that some time ago had traced a ring around the moon. And the moon was round and red, stained with the blood of the sun hidden behind the mountains. And from the moment of disintegration, the bitter sensation that all was lost irrevocably and forever.

six

I truly loved them. I would have given my life for them and honored their eternal presence; I'd have made others honor it as well, like little Saint Dominick of Val, the Holy Guardian Infant, Saint Mary Goretti, all the Innocents and Martyrs who in all their glory had sacrificed everything for the faith. I was deeply moved when reading those short biographies in the *Lives of the Roman Martyrs*, or the "Exemplary Lives" comic books in the Novarro series that Brother Marcos de La Iglesia Vicario gave me so that I would be like the martyrs. Youthful heroism, renunciation, purity, and innocence were virtues I admired and valued more than all the others because I knew I lacked them. I identified with the martyrs' early sufferings, a little like mine but infinitely more sublime, and I so yearned to have their faith, integrity, constancy, because more than anything, I wanted to be like them; yet I couldn't, I would never be. In the soul of a little black boy like me, an animal in the wild, the vices of my primitive race were locked in, just as Father Amadeo had told me in confession—Father Amadeo was a priest who had come to replace Father Ortiz during his six months of absence, and the one who refused to absolve my sins. Only He in his infinite mercy would have been capable of freeing me from my heavy burdens and feeble spirit, only the One who had cured dropsy and leprosy, the One who had brought Lazarus back to life.

I'll never know why, because no one ever told me, but I guessed it was the hand of Providence that had given me physical features resembling those of Father Ortiz. What is certain is that when I passed the exam with flying colors and received a certificate for completing elementary school, when Don Ramón danced with joy in front of my father, and the school inspector congratulated him for the excellent preparation of his students, my father decided to send me to missionary school in the district capital. It was a huge building with a large, comfortable lobby; we wanted to cool off there but we weren't allowed. There was a grand patio where the bad boys were sent to cut weeds as punishment; it was surrounded by coffee groves, where we worked harvesting the coffee beans. My arm still sways with the cutting motion of the machete, swift, precise strokes at the base of the plants, my body stiff, my back bent, the smell of the soft soil, the red earth of Guinea. The air was filled with the smell of chlorophyll, moist earth, and a dissected earthworm hanging from the leaves. Father Remigio María Echenagusia, the one we called Hot-Eye because his eyes were always blinking nervously, blood-shot from parasites and from his constant bad humor. He was an old and vigorous missionary, he stilled loved physical exercise, looking strong even in comparison to the brawniest blacks in the vicinity, he said so himself, he always won, it's true, and we admired him because of it, no one was stronger than Hot-Eye , but I think now that they all let him win because they were scared of his rage, because he was a missionary who neither allowed nor forgave any challenge to his authority as Father Superior. This time I was determined to respond to the immense confidence my father had in me, and I managed to fulfill his wish for me as a model student, especially in the first months. My awkward phrases in Latin, or what looked like Latin, and the enthusiastic recommendation of Father Ortiz paved the way, it's true—also Father Hot-Eye chose me as his altar boy. At first, I loved masses for the dead, especially when they were sung, the solemnity Father Hot-Eye gave to those dark moments. He looked sad but proud in his black cassock and his white rochet starched by the nuns from the school in front of ours where my sister was a boarding student. I never visited her because the boys weren't allowed to visit the girls, not even if they were our sisters. And that bony yet beautiful Sister Juana was always spying when they went to rosary in their green uniforms, eager to catch an exchange of leering glances. And when the priest sat down at the head of the coffin flanked by burning candles and recited the words of the requiem, *aeternam dona eis Domine et lux perpetua luceat eis*, and Esteban and I chimed in, very mournfully, *libera me Domine de mortem aeternam in dia irae tremendis*, I looked at the few blacks standing on the benches. Esteban's father was always among them, a very devout man who always prayed at night; the priest seemed to be mourning more than they were. At first I wanted to see the faces of the dead, having never seen a dead person, but later I felt a tremendous animosity toward them. I understood why the priest stepped up the pace of these requiem masses, he even prohibited them to be sung, because some of the deceased blacks already smelled, a much stronger odor than when they were alive. It was penetrating: like the smell of Marcelino Mba Nsamio, whose wives didn't want to bring him to church when he died because they said he had been baptized when he was unconscious and at the point of death, and after the catechist finally managed to convince them that his baptism was as valid as the ones performed at birth, his belly was so swollen that it was very difficult to close the coffin. Four blacks had to sit on the wooden casket while another one nailed it shut. And when Father Hot-Eye began to sprinkle the ceremonial incense over him, praying for the Lord to receive the soul of his servant Marcelino, Don Marcelino went puff! and the chapel was filled with the smell of death, and even Esteban's father had to hold his nose with his devout fingers. And Esteban had to bring another incensory to the sacristy because I couldn't spoon enough incense onto the hot coals to hide the overpowering smell of the deceased Don Marcelino. And of course his wives fled from the church, saying no wonder, they knew that the Lord would never receive a lecher who on top of it all had been baptized without even knowing it, and from then on the church had a lingering smell of incense mixed with rotten flesh. And that was how Don Marcelino Maria Mba Nsamio became a legend, buried with a black cloth with a yellow cross on it covering his coffin, because no one dared deny him an honor deserved in such an original way. When a few weeks later the Colonial Police Instructor was killed with a machete by his disloyal servant, or so they said, and a flag was draped over his coffin, people were not surprised by what they believed had happened to the Police Instructor, not even by the sad misfortune awaiting the disloyal servant, who suffered the horrendous justice of the garrote. No, they thought it all had to do with the ordeal of Don Marcelino, who ended up with a funeral worthy of a white dignitary. The only difference was that the flag covering his remains was black and not multicolored, which makes perfect sense, doesn't it?

And every Thursday, Father Remigio Maria Echenagusia, Esteban, and I climbed in the Peugeot truck owned by the mission and went around the neighboring villages to buy food for all the boarding students. These weekly excursions were fun for me; they satisfied my wanderlust and curiosity and allowed me to verify Father Hot-Eye's fondness for me. The *tumba* drum spread the news of our arrival from town to town; it was a wooden cylinder set on a mahogany pedestal in the middle of a cluster of pineapple trees. One of the trunks had been hollowed out by fire, creating a vertical crevice that allowed it to produce two harmonizing sounds. Our presence was announced so the people in the next village could prepare for the priest's visit. Civilization had found an edifying use of the tribes' age-old practices of calling for battle with the occupiers. Detachments of warriors hidden in the darkness could hear footsteps in the damp silence of the night; it was a coded death sentence, the messages of the *tumba* were secret, not everyone could decipher them—not even the native traitors who sold themselves to the occupiers by serving as guides—especially if the drum sounds were produced by the expert hands of the shaman in charge of protecting the tribe. And now the only sorcerer was Father Remigio Maria Echenagusia, who was welcomed joyfully; no one dared withdraw from the call of the *tumba*. The sorcerer held the amulet in his pink fingers and took note of its history while the new witch doctor thrashed out the names of the dying, the neophytes, and the catechumens, and each one of them took the precaution of offering gifts to the sorcerer before the ceremony, honorable gifts, however simple: from one a white plate, from another a red hen, from yet another a pregnant sheep, from some even their children, so that they would be educated by the science of the Lord. The power of the sorcerer was infinite, he acted with the conviction of his sanctifying mission, as much a believer as his victims.

And as he took confession from the dying and signed baptismal papers for the recently converted and the catechumens and gave marriage certificates to those expecting a church wedding, Esteban and I remained quiet and solemn, keeping close watch on the Peugeot truck. This was what was expected of us, apprentices and perpetrators of his triumph over the tribe. He always came back in a hurry, giving orders to unload the truck filled with the spoils of his magic: sacks of yucca and *malanga*, bunches of bananas and plantains, baskets of peanuts, pieces of salted fish and smoked fish—all this had fallen into the insatiable belly of the Peugeot. And on top of the mound of booty, cages of hens and ducks were tied to the truck so they wouldn't fall off and break, adding an unreal musicality to the deafening roar of the vehicle driven by Father Hot-Eye. His expression was sometimes beatific, sometimes resolute, mostly sour, but he was always whistling a song to the Virgin of Begonia. Sitting close by his side, I tried not to get in his way as he shifted gears abruptly and neatly; I got as close as I could to Esteban without being indecent. The priest always had his eyes glued to the window as he tried to count the number of crosses in the cemeteries we kept sweeping by; they were numerical proof of the high rate of Christianization in each village we left in the dust. And when he stepped on the break unexpectedly—a naked child crossing the road without looking where he was going, or some goats ruminating calmly in the middle of a curve—my body brushing against his dusty white cassock, I was overcome with a sudden feeling of guilt as I stared through the windshield at the winding, unpaved road. And I thought about the naked families carrying all their belongings on their heads, walking silently, constantly pursued by a swarm of flies, while the priest honked his horn to shoo them out of the way. Or I would look at the men hunched over at the edge of the road, clearing the grass with little hoes and filling the ruts with dirt. They were supervised by a third boss with his arms crossed, affirming his authority and doffing his cap as Father Echenagusia went by—it was a cap adorned by a shiny brass eagle, symbol of the Empire. Or the woman bent double under fifty kilos of boiled yucca hanging painfully from a chord tied to her forehead like the yoke of a beast of burden. Or the young mother, still a child, with her infant wrapped in banana leaves, eyes squinting under the weakest ray of the sun. We passed by bamboo huts exposed to the midday glare. And from out of the meeting houses, old men appeared with curly white beards, their feet weighted to the ground by elephantiasis, like gigantic *egombegombe* roots, circling around mats of bamboo as they prepared to replace the roof, and in their dark eyes was the deepest sadness.

Together all of us boarding students unloaded the truck and carried the goods into the storage area. From there, Brother Marcos de la Iglesia Vicario gathered enough provisions to feed us twice a week, although he didn't prepare our food but only cooked for Father Hot-Eye and Father Ortiz when the latter was not out in the vicinity of his apostolic mission. The catechumens and the girl boarders served peanut soup almost every day except Sunday, when they seasoned it with bits of salted fish. The women lived in large rustic cabins on the other side of the church: the catechumens, fat women, old and pious before they were baptized, and the *sixas*, mischievous ladies, happy and confident, who were as old as forty before they were married, all of them busy in the affairs of the cabins, attending daily classes on home economics and hygiene. I don't know what else the nuns taught them, but they also went to evening catechism classes taught by Father Hot-Eye and all the religious functions. In addition, they worked the land that belonged to the nuns on the other side of the road, swept the school floors and the chapel, washed our short pants, and cooked us peanut soup, and maybe in the afternoon you could catch a glimpse of them winking at one of the older male boarders. How flighty they were, breaking the seventh commandment even before the holy sacrament of matrimony. The food at school wasn't exactly delicious, I knew it, and I told my mother, but my father answered, my son, life is a vale of tears, you must endure it as much as you can in order to be an honorable man. Mommy, I don't like it here, I've got stomachache, it hurts, and I don't like the food; and a few days later there was my father with a jar of medicine for tapeworm. Take it after every meal, son, you must take the medicine no matter how much you hate it, it's very good, Don Santos Casamitjana gave it to me, it can't be bad if he says his own kids take it. Father, I've been feeling sick for days, please excuse me from serving Mass today. I've heard that before, you lazy boy, what you want is to stay in bed, get up now, lately you've been behaving badly, the next time I see your dad, I'll tell him, let's see if he knocks some sense into you. My son, what's wrong, you're so thin? Nothing mom. Maybe you're not getting enough food. No mom. Well, eat everything they serve you, and don't make a face when you look at it. Yes, yes mom. The food was terrible, but no one dared complain ever since that legendary day when Father Remigio Maria Echenagusia broke Silverio Ondo Mesocoo's nose. Silverio Ondo was the son of the first chief of the powerful Esamatua tribe; he had had a curse put on him by a great sorcerer. Indeed, he ended up poisoned and strangled by a boa constrictor exactly twenty-four hours after being expelled from school for complaining about the poor quality of the food. And as a result, Father Superior's prestige grew so much that all the tribes in the area nullified the power of their own sorcerers and shamans and converted to Catholicism because the priest's powers had proved infinitely more effective than those of the supposedly powerful chief of the powerful Esamatua, whose useless babble and feeble threats were never of any consequence. Father Hot-Eye took advantage of the circumstances to instill fear in the bodies of the unbelieving, disobedient, and unruly blacks. This is how he sealed his authority, so unquestionable that the Reverend Bishop and Apostolic Prefect of the entire island of Fernando Poo, who resided in the capital of Santa Isabel, named him Father Superior for all time, and his authority became indisputable; his witchcraft was powerful, and even though some of the elders insisted on curbing the feverish wave of baptisms as they tried to counter the arguments of the believers, they dared not challenge the priest directly—they were afraid of ending up like the legendary Silverio Ondo Mesocoo. And from then on, the priest was venerated with the same devotion as the image of Saint Michael the Archangel, with his sword raised high, his boot on Satan's head; you could see the icon from the first altar of the church under a velvet canopy. And to everyone in the area, all the elders together looked like the figure of the defeated Satan, tongue hanging out, incisors long and pointed, hungry for human flesh, horns of an antelope, a terrible grotesque scowl on his face, and despite the pain and humiliation there was still a certain arrogance in him, the horrid sin that had taken him to the flaming darkness from which he was trying to escape.

And that image was engraved in my memory forever. The peanut soup prepared by the catechumens that night was particularly insipid; at least the younger ones, who were being groomed for marriage, took care to put a little salt in it or grind the peanuts thoroughly, but the catechumens made their soup white and lumpy, maybe because they were getting old and tired; others said it was because they were frigid old witches. Felipe Nculu had just placed the missal on the lectern, and as we ate supper in rigorous silence, someone read a chapter from *The Complete Works of Father Coloma*. I had just peeled the yucca, and in the middle of it was a huge centipede, it was as long and red as a boiled lobster. Our collective reaction—surprise, repulsion, screams, and retches—ripped into the silence of the night, alarming the priest, who hurried over to our table, and without expression, without compassion, he punished us right at that moment by making us eat the yucca in absolute silence, all of it except the centipede. My vomit was the same as everyone else's at the table, the insect in the center of the brass plate like a gloomy mummy wrapped in yucca, its color contrasting with the whiteness. Father Hot-eye shouted at us to eat, but we were as proud as Satan: we didn't obey. I wondered whether I would be the only Fang in the history of my people to eat centipede, and that frightened me more than anything; how can a Fang eat that, there's no respect for anyone who acts like an animal in the jungle, and what's life for, if others don't respect you? Insults were raining on us now, we barely understood them, but I could make out the priest's contorted, angry face, as red as the boiled centipede in the yucca. He ordered us to eat, but no one did; it's not disobedience, Father, we can't even pick up the spoon and dip it into the peanut soup with puke in it, let alone the fork and stab it into the yucca laced with centipede liquid. The priest didn't listen, he kept on shouting; as if in a dream I saw his saliva drip onto my neck like the first drops of rain, and then I felt the blow on my right ear. I remember staggering, I managed to grab onto the table before falling down on the floor; down with me came the puke-filled soup dish and the plate with the yucca and the centipede, still enormous, still red. The priest kept on yelling recklessly as his black shoes landed on my buttocks, my shoulders and my head. I saw his foot coming toward my face, I curled up like an anteater, but I didn't have the anteater's scales for protection, I felt the blow, and another kick on the back of my hand, his cassock brushing over me with every convulsive movement. My silence exasperated him, I imagine he would have wanted me to cry out, begging forgiveness, but I said nothing, not even ouch, and he kept on kicking me harder and more out of control. He was still yelling; sometimes I could figure out the words like unruly, gypsy, pirate, loafers, Sierra Morena hooligans, again and again in an endless list, and with growing pain in my rib cage, I jumped to my feet and ran to the door of the dining room, trying to reach the darkness of the corridor before he grabbed me by the collar.

I wandered around the patio, whimpering in pain and rage, strangled by powerlessness in the face of injustice, a terrible doubt lingering in my conscience, my guardian angel reproaching my arrogance and pride as the fallen angel consoled me: you did very well, when has anyone eaten a boiled centipede in the middle of a yucca? that priest is cruel, don't ever pay attention to him again. And I strolled over to the church, opened the door to the sacristy, and continued through the altar boy's entrance; I knelt down in front of the sacrarium and begged for all the forgiveness in heaven. The church was filled with an intense silence, like the pain in my heart. No consolation, no miracle. The candles cast a faint light on the face of Satan, who looked as if he were smiling at me from under the Archangel's boot. The darkness was ominous, filled with dancing shadows, but in spite of it all I could distinguish the silhouette of Brother Marcos de la Iglesia Vicario coming toward me from the sacristy. He took me by the shoulders, but I didn't get up. It was either his comforting complicity or his smell of garlic that broke my resistance, for while he was accompanying me back to the dormitory, he scrutinized me anxiously. He was just as afraid of the disquieting presence of Father Superior as I was. And only two sentiments remain of that long convalescence: the terrible certainty that my father was not on my side, and my failure to get closer to them. In spite of it all I wanted to love them, and when I was older I even wanted to be like them.

seven

Tío Abeso was sitting in his seat of honor; the back of the seat was braided with *melongo,* and on the top was a carved alligator, its jaws wide open and its long row of wooden teeth looking as though they were about to stroke my uncle's white hair. The midday sun, crystal clear and sparkling, penetrated the lushness of all the leaves that encircled his town: banana, plantain, *atanga,* mango, papaya, orange. And the breeze blew threw through all four sides of the meeting house, filling it with a sweet smell of ripe pineapple. Tío Abeso, in all his magical and mysterious dignity, gazed at my father, who was sitting at his left on a bamboo bed, his face in his hands, looking strange and humble just like me. On his right was Tío Meco, who had come from far away for this occasion; his large, tattooed face was proud, sweat shone on his bald apostolic head, his feet were bare, and the big toe of his right foot was sketching a humanoid figure on the dusty floor. Tío Abeso's eyes were lost now in the horizon, a close horizon due to the greenery in all its exuberance; his gaze reached beyond the jungle. Who knows, perhaps it reached the ancestors as he begged them for protection, balance, and wisdom to reconcile the situation that had arisen because of me. A wasp buzzing around the meeting house was suddenly still, the leaves were quiet on the trees, a duck lay asleep at my feet.

I had just described for them, for the fiftieth time that day, the cause of my problem at the missionary school. They made me repeat all of it several times, over and over; I had been at home for almost a month, and my body no longer hurt; every day I had to explain it to them. They were elderly people, very prudent, and they needed to be sure that I hadn't contradicted myself and wasn't adding or omitting things from one version to another; it was also possible that they wanted me to keep these events in my memory forever so I could tell my future grandchildren about them, I don't know; and when they were absolutely sure that I was telling the truth, they gathered to reach a decision. During my convalescence I had come to believe my father did not love me, that's the truth; how could he doubt my word if he didn't even want to listen to me? But now I no longer believe it was his natural inclination that led him to interrupt me at every moment telling me that something wasn't true, Father Echenagusia told me you are the ringleader of a conspiracy to destroy his authority. We can't administer a boarding school of a hundred or so students without authority or discipline, because we are here to civilize, and to civilize means literally to cure, to eliminate the panic complex,

to rid all of you of your telluric psychosis, you understand; this is
why our work requires that we first penetrate the indigenous soul
right through to the subsoil, to the remote depths from which the
monstrous and deformed emerge like maggots, as in the paintings
of Hieronymus Bosch, their anarchic and crumbling conceptions,
you understand? And I was sure my father had not understood Echenagusia's lecture except that I was the ringleader of a conspiracy
to subvert his sacred authority. And of course, he blamed me for the
absolute evil, or that's how I thought it was during my recuperation,
a type of evil comparable only to the sickness and heat in the imagination of Bosch. Who is this Bosch, son? Well, I don't know, papa.
Could it be Saint John Bosch? I don't think so, because if it were, he
wouldn't be a saint. That's true, of course, and he repeated the priest's
lively sermons to my uncles. And Tío Abeso snorted with contempt,
shook his head, and brought a handful of tobacco to his mouth. He
chewed slowly, drowning out the buzz of a bee, and my father continued, unwittingly imitating Father Echenagusia's intonation, picking away at the arguments. Consider the tremendous responsibility
on the shoulders of these men of God, they have come from very far
away only for our good, because we live better now than when I was a
child; you yourself, Abeso, taught us to respect our elders because the
elderly represent wisdom, you did this harshly, don't deny it, you were
our father and you educated us; I remember when you locked me
in the house for two days for laughing at an old man who trembled
like a dry leaf every time he began to speak—his name was Nguema
Olinga, remember? This is why discipline is so important for a man,

respect for the elderly, dignity, judgment; I understand those men of God who must educate more than a hundred of those boys who aren't even their children, because we blacks respect no laws except brute strength, our character is infantile like unruly children impossible to set them on the straight and narrow; we have a flimsy impressionable spirit, the only thing that daunts us and makes us take the straight path is energy, firmness, justice, and above all strength; it's good to treat a boy as a loving friend, but when that treatment becomes excessive, if bad behavior is rewarded, if they are not severely punished when they deserve it, since they can't tell the difference, they imagine we're scared of them, and they despise those who don't know how to rule by force. And my father had even acquired Father Echenagusia's tone of voice, his manner, everything.

I saw Tío Meco's facial muscles contracting, he was slapping himself hard on the cheek trying to kill flies that were going after him, and he looked at his open hand, and with the fingers of his other hand he grabbed a wing of the crushed fly, he threw it on the ground, and he finished it off by stepping on it with his big toe, and he cleaned off the little puddle of blood left on his hand on his pant leg at the same level as his knee. Then he scratched the bite, firmly establishing his body's balance. And he stared at my father, trying to recover the thread of his exposition, elliptical and monotonous, the train of thought that was lost due to the constant irritation of the flies. And my father was there with his mouth shut and his face buried in his hands, rubbing his chin, just like Father Echenagusia. He observed a swarm of ants carrying a large piece of banana toward their nest;

the opening to which appeared as a black speck in the yellow dust near one of the three stones that marked the hearth at the center of the meeting house. The embers had burned out; what remained was a mound of ashes awaiting cousin Micue, who was in charge of the daily cleaning. She always had her head in the clouds; the older she grew, the sloppier she became, which was why no man would put up with her. Tío Abeso was fidgeting on his seat of honor, he picked his nose with the little finger of his left hand and loudly spit out an enormous brown wad of chewed tobacco, and when the substance faded into the dust of the floor, forming little islands of mud, the bits of tobacco were left exposed like the pebbles in a brook at dry season. He criticized my father for not listening to me, and said that my father only believed the white man's version. Every conflict has two sides, and every man of honor would consider both of them before judging, and you are not being fair because you refuse to see one of those sides, just like them. This child learned how to deal with them from an early age, and he knows the whites better than we do; he understands their language better than anyone, and he has read their books and knows their ways. This little one is wise, and for that he deserves our respect; I taught you to respect the elderly because they are wise, not because they are old. An old person who doesn't act like an old person isn't worthy of respect. And I, much older than all of you, respect this boy of yours because he has both the wisdom of the tribe and the wisdom of the whites inside him, though I acknowledge the effort it's costing him.

I couldn't look into his face. His eyes gave out a special glow, his face had widened, and his immense power was so tangible I could see it emanating from his bare torso, his powerful arm, his right index finger always straight but not accusing like my father's when he imitated Father Echenagusia; it emitted a measured justice, an indispensable reflection of his age-old wisdom and unrivaled authority. And I understood that Tío Abeso's authority was great because he was able to silence my father and Uncle Meco, who behaved like us when they scolded us. It was then that I realized I was not sure about Tío Abeso, a lack of confidence arising from deep respect and love, and it made me ashamed: How can I question my only model? And I felt bad about it, I couldn't look into his shining face with that special glow; forgive me, uncle, I won't let rumors wear down the confidence I have in you. And in the cloudless sky, a hawk was soaring and soaring in concentric circles and descending majestically with its wings spread, its eyes fixed on chickens pecking at the ground in the patio. Its shadow was the danger sign, and the little chicks scattered as the hens began to squawk, their necks rigid, pointing toward the sky. The hawk climbed high enough to gather the strength he needed to make the last circle before his quick straight descent onto the chick that had not found its way to shelter. We all yelled at once, *kua, kua*, clapping *kua, kua*, the chorus of screams frightened the hawk, and its claws let go its prey, and our screams continued, *kua, kua*, and our clapping as well; the hawk turned in the air and again came down toward the falling chick like a dive-bomber and grabbed it just before it hit the ground. It was all so beautiful and sad at the same time. It had never occurred to me that some things could be beautiful and sad at once, like the love of the tribe or the love of something impossible, and I clearly understood it was a premonition, and Tío Abeso's eyes asked if I had grasped it, and my eyes answered yes, that I had understood all of it. Because something ominous was circling over the tribe, an ominous aura around the moon, and it would overcome the weak, the timid, and the inept, all who were not wholly useful to the tribe, and a stream of dust traced the circle made by the hawk now lost above the highest branches of the guava trees, and we were no longer yelling and clapping. And Tío Abeso kept right on talking as if nothing had happened, nature had accomplished its mission, the weak succumb to the claws of the strong and everything stays the same, and my uncle said he would never understand the exercise of power. Power is above all pain, feeling what the governed feel, knowing how to endure, this is what chief Abeso Motulu taught me; the heart of a chief should be the sum total of the hearts of all those under his protection. Even those who are always bickering, always violent, especially toward the little ones, when all is said and done it's because they are afraid. And we know they are afraid, and this gives us a great advantage, so all we need to do is discover the source of their power, how they got to where they are, how they construct their boats, and what they do to preserve their food for so long without rotting, and how they manage to preseve the energy of lightening and fire, and when we discover this, you'll see how we will triumph over them, because on our side we have shrewdness and patience.

And he stared at me with his sympathetic look, with a gaze only he and I knew; don't despair, his eyes were telling me; you have

125

the power of the ancestors, and they will always protect you, here, there, now, always, because you have been anointed with the essence of the tribe's power; the tribe sees itself in you. And it looked as though Great-grandfather Motulu Mbenga was also looking at me from the highest branches of the guava tree, and he told me a man doesn't cry. You shouldn't cry, because crying is the last thing; we shall fight them; our resistance begins now; they prevailed because they had the wisdom of their gods. We must penetrate the secrets of the white man's magic, so that we have the same material as they do, and then they will be defeated because we have the fortitude of those who have left and the energy of those who are here; if they tell you to eat centipede, eat centipede, because they don't know your obedience will be your strength; if they tell you to run on all fours, run on all fours, because they don't know that your obedience will be your strength; if they tell you to kill, kill, because they don't know that this act will be our strength, that it will help us defeat them later and return glory to the tribe. Do all they ask until you have acquired the formula for their power, and bring it to the tribe, and then they will be conquered. And my father too was looking at me lovingly, and then I understood his role. He had never been on their side, he was the link between the tribe and the occupiers, someone has to negotiate: Someone has to talk to them to figure out how they should be treated, what foods they like and what bothers them, how they fornicate and how many cigarettes they smoke a day; someone should be with them to spy on them from the inside; the tribe must store information on their movements and their ideas. And that morning

I understood, without anyone having to tell me, through the eyes of my father, through his stern and tender face that spoke to me without speaking: you must be strong, my son, to be a honorable man in this life. And Tío Meco confirmed it: carry on, as the toe of his right foot sketched strange humanoid figures on the dusty floor and then, exasperated, wiped them out only to begin again; carry on, don't abandon us now, you are our only hope for acquiring their formulas; they have consecrated you with their wisdom and their esteem, they say you're a smart boy and they only want smart boys around them; you must get inside them to possess their formulas for the sake of the tribe. And they all spoke to me that way without speaking, and I listened to them without hearing, and I was very afraid: How was I going to get inside them without being seen? I'll be found out, and things will get even worse.

And then the haughty image of Father Ortiz appeared to me, adorned in his sacred ornaments, baptizing children and opening the doors of eternity to them with his words, listening to the most intimate secrets through confession. How can he not be powerful when he knows us better than anyone, touching the Baby Jesus, the Redeemer, with his delicate cherry hands, converting water into wine and wine into blood, and I remembered the bloody body of the instructor, who they said was hacked to death by a disloyal servant with a machete, being brought into the church draped with the colored flag, and Father Echenagusia sprinkling incense with the hyssop. And I understood his power, the immense power of the priest, the sorcerer of his tribe before whom all others would kneel and kiss his hand; even Brother Marcos de la Iglesia Vicario kissed his hand and cooked his food although he dressed in a cassock just like him; even Señor Casamitjana with all his money and his trading post filled with cans of sardines and bottles of olive oil and his great power over my father and Policarpo the trading-post clerk, even Casamitjana would go to church every Sunday and holy days of obligation and would discreetly place a fifty-peseta bill on the collection plate Esteban held out to everybody, unlike the others who would throw a one-peseta coin into the plate from a distance so that it would make a noise and everyone would see how generous they were; and Señora M M would come by with her heels clacking rhythmically in her untouchable white-woman ways, and she would kneel down devout and contrite and modest right at the foot of the altar, and she would open her red mouth to receive the Sacred Host from the fingers of the priest, and I would tap the communion tray on her throat to let her know I understood. And sometimes she could not hold back her ticklishness and she smiled with her eyes closed, and the priest surely thought it was because she was so happy to receive the Lord; what a pious woman, a real saint; but Señora M M knew of my devotion to her and that was our secret, and I was sure she was glad that I liked her, because when she left church she always gave me candy and told my mother what a nice boy I was. And all this was created by the mysterious power of the priest, sorcerer of his tribe; he was the most powerful, there was no doubt about it, and a bit of his magical and mysterious power had rubbed off on me, because I could dress up in the red cassock and white surplice and touch the chalice on the outside with my black hands and unfold the corporal cloth and dry my little fingers with the purifier and transport the chrisom with the magical ointment that resurrected the dead and let the dying see the eyes of God. It's true, I too participated in all that mysterious and magical power in spite of my early life of an unforgivable sinner, and I couldn't help listening to the call of Father Ortiz dressed for solemn Mass sung in Gregorian chant, and at that very moment I saw myself in the banana grove, not now but in the future, dressed in the white cassock and the great white surplice starched by the generous thin hands of Sister Juana, who was so beautiful, and with my straight fingers shining with sacramental oil I traced a cross on the wrinkled tattooed face of Tío Abeso kneeling at my feet: Santiago Bulu Abeso Motulu, *ab renuntias Satanas?* and my uncle and my father and my mother and Mama Andeme and everyone would answer as all the natives answered, *abronunsio, et omnibus pompis eius?, abronunsio, et omnibus pecatis eius?, abronunsio,* and I would rub his white head with holy water, *Santiago Bulu Abeso Motulu ego te baptizo in nomine Patris, et Filiis, et Spiritus Sancti, amen,* and then I would win the salvation of the tribe because all the tribe would then be converted to the One True Faith. And without a second thought, I got up slowly, cleared my throat, and requested permission to speak. Tío Abeso looked at me intently, my father sat up straight in his bamboo chair, and Tío Meco's big toe stopped drawing humanoid figures so that he could give his utmost attention to my words: I want to be a priest, I told them, and then I was silent.

They were paralyzed, mouths open, shocked, afraid, do you remember? For they never imagined you would say those words. Tío Abeso got up from his seat of honor crowned by the alligator; he spit out a wad of tobacco and went over to you, looking grave, and you got up ready to run, an unspeakable fear had come into you. You thought he was going to strike you, and there was no reason to be afraid, he never hit you nor would he ever, but you tended to express your respect for the elders through panic, that's what they had managed to create in you. And my uncle stood there in front of you, looked into your eyes, and you looked into his with the fireflies twinkling in them. And in your own were the spirits of the ancestors speaking through your eyes, you saw them and you recognized them, and they told Tío Abeso that you had spoken to give voice to his designs, and he understood that he could do nothing but accept the will of the ancestors. But he made you repeat those words, and you did it: I'm asking permission to become a priest. And then Tío Abeso said that important words required important decisions, and important decisions should be thought over; now go play, my son, and leave us alone, because the elders must discuss this among ourselves; we must call on your Grandfather Nguema Anseme.

But you didn't go out to play. The immense devotion that had long been accumulating in your spirit, faith you thought had burned out when in fact it had only become still, blossomed once again. And you went to your bedroom, which was empty, so you filled it with rosaries and figures of saints, and you found the old *Little Prayer Book* gnawed away by mice, and the old notebooks, and the *Dalmau Car-les Pla Encyclopedia* taken out of its cover, and the tarnished copy of *Djoba Nguema and Bokesa*, and among the worn pages of the *Little Prayer Book* a cockroach emerged; you swept it off for daring to curse the sacred book moistened by your tears. And you recited the final vespers prayer, *ut videas filios filiorum tuorum pax super Israel*, and peace came to you; you placed the book on the lectern on the night table, converted again into an altar; you went over to the edge of the banana grove and dug out a little hole. And there it was, miraculously intact, all wrapped up, and you opened it with infinite devotion and buried it under the table cloth as if it were a sacrificial mantel on which you placed all your relics and all the offerings destined to convert the tribe. You didn't say Mass this time but stood still with your hands together in sincere devotion; you no longer expected miracles, because you were turning into a skeptic even though you wouldn't realize it for many, many years, on the other side of the ocean. And for the first time you prayed with calculated devotion, rational and mature, and you prayed to the Lord to enlighten your spirit so that you might reach your predestined goal, and you prayed for forgiveness of all your sins, committed not through an evil impulse but through weakness, a weakness you hoped would be overcome with the aid of His infinite mercy. You were at peace: when you got up and brushed the dust off your knees, you felt good, comforted, protected by the power of God and the power of the tribe. And when Father Ortiz came by that Saturday afternoon and you asked for confession, you knew He would forgive you. Father Ortiz understood; he knew you were beginning to leave your childhood behind, and his words of consolation were destined for his own salvation through yours. For he had always considered you a smart lad and couldn't allow, as he would later tell your father, walking under a full moon, that an earnest soul like yours should go astray when it was meant for the highest of designs, and that he would feel worthy if his apostolic mission had been crowned by a sincere vocation that would yield a new pastor for the Lord's flock. I baptized him, he said to my father as their silhouettes stood out under the light of the moon, and my utmost satisfaction would be to take part in his ordination; he is a sensitive and devout soul, there's no doubt he has been touched by the grace of the Lord. And when your father—more as an attempt to convince himself than as a real disagreement—objected that you were only a child, Father, can't you see this may be just an illusion; how can we be so sure that what you say is true? (in his African accent). The priest answered, full of confidence, don't worry, he's already thirteen years old, and at that age one knows what one wants in life; at age thirteen I too entered the seminary, if he insists on being a priest we can't oppose the will of God with our poor human vision. But Father, don't you remember that a few years ago it looked as though he wanted to be a priest and then he forgot how to pray. It may not last long but only be something passing; besides, he acts...Don't fret about his behavior, its absolutely normal, he has doubted, that indicates his vocation is sincere and his spirit is thoughtful; the Lord only enlightens our soul; everyone chooses his own path, and each decides whether to follow the call or not, and it takes time to decide, especially in an atmosphere like this; your home is exemplary, but temptation is everywhere and bad company as well; even in the home a family relationship can turn into a sinful one by an act of the devil, which is why you must do everything to prevent your closest relatives from coming into your home if they haven't been married according to the mandates of the Holy Mother Church, and your son must enter the seminary as soon as possible so that he'll be free of the impure influences of this atmosphere; I'll see that he gets admitted into the Seminary in Banapa for the next school year, where he will be in a proper atmosphere for study and prayer, and now let us pray to the Lord, our Father who art in heaven.

And the months passed by, and you helped Ambrosio the catechist decipher the teachings of the Gospels and the meaning of Advent and what Saint Paul was telling us in that paragraph of his Third Epistle to the Thessalonians. And every morning during the Ave Maria you watched cousin Paco playing the *tumba*, and every night you said the rosary in your family's house, and you gave your little brother a stern glance as he dozed while kneeling on the cold cement floor next to you. At times you were the one who led the family in saying the rosary, delegated by your father and elevated as firstborn to the supreme category of only son, or in your father's absence, as when he had gone to the Indigenous Authority to renew his rifle license or to register the birth of a new member of the family to ensure that he would be emancipated forever. Because your father had won his freedom through his work and continuous contact with the occupiers in his mission as a spy on the tribe's activities. And on the Sundays when Father Ortiz didn't come, after Ambrosio's long sermon you stayed in the chapel with the boys and girls, and you organized them into separate groups to review the catechism or to seal their weak faith, or to learn to praise the Lord through song; you said, and now we are going to review the one that goes "blessed be your purity," and you stood in front of the choirs and led the devotions, sung melodiously and devoutly, almost mystically; that's good, and when Father comes we'll sing this one, and now the Salve Mater, let's see, very good—hey, you, don't laugh, Mbo, we're not playing now, whoever doesn't want to learn to praise the Lord with song should leave the chapel; here we must pay due respect to the sacred presence of the Redeemer, is that clear once and for all? And your authority and power were becoming more entrenched as the months passed, and everyone respected you and loved you: look at him, he's going to be such a good priest, he already walks and tilts his head like Father Ortiz. Next Sunday we're going to sing Praise Be the Most Blessed Saint; let's see, you, Mincue, give us a note, and when I go like this the girls will join followed by the boys; and you raised your hand, you, Ba, your voice is shrill, lower it, now you sing solo, when Micue gets to the Sacramento, you begin, good, that's right, that's the way we sang it in school. And all those energetic gestures made you tired, and all that singing in different notes so that they could follow; these little blacks will never learn, remember? they must work harder, that's the only way we'll make wholesome people out of them, and teaching them the fear of God through the liturgy of the One True Holy Church, solemn and edifying, this was what was needed, you thought. And after the choir practice when Tía Te came by to ask you something, you slipped away mysteriously, I have to say vespers now, and then the end prayer and then the rosary and then ejaculatories, don't bother me, I have to pray, you said, remembering the words of Father Ortiz: don't let yourself be trapped, stay clear of female corruption, the best way to do it is to keep yourself busy at all times, because idleness is the mother of vice.

Every day, Don Ramón arrived at your house full of himself; he and your father would sit and chat about you, that you would be the first seminarian in the whole region, chosen by God to convert the heathens, and when you are far away from here remember that I taught you your first letters, it's true. Yes, Don Ramón, that's true, he's so well educated, he owes it to you, his teacher, only a man with your wisdom could infuse such education in these children. And Don Ramón was flattered; how many times in his life had his ego been inflated at your expense, and he looked at you delighted: I always knew this boy would go far. And you went into the patio to shut yourself out; you didn't see all the looks they gave you, your father, your mother, everybody. Happiness has come back to this child; now I'm sure he will be an honorable man in life. He won't let me down, I'm proud of him, and you should also be proud, woman, a man of God has come out of your womb, a man who will liberate us from the torments of hell. I'll never be able to say confession to him, how could I tell my sins to my own son? Don't be foolish, woman, don't you see he will no longer be your son, that he's a messenger sent by God. How could we have spanked a messenger of God? I'm sure that's a sin. Well, I don't think so, I'm sure Saint Joseph hit Jesus a couple of times when he was a boy, but he's still a saint.

And that's how your father and mother whispered as they saw you stroll around the patio all contrite and withdrawn, with rosary beads in your fingers and the *Little Prayer Book* under your arm; you knew they were happy, and your happiness was theirs; you were no longer a mere firstborn, you had risen to the category of only son; the other brothers were of no consequence now because all the aspirations of your mother and father centered on you. And you prayed to God for the preservation of that expression of fulfillment in their faces, and for the strength never to let them down again, so that they could have a bit of contentment on earth.

eight

And Grandfather Nguema Anseme woke you, touching you three times on the forehead. You rubbed your eyes and saw his smiling face. He unfolded the white *clote* for you—you barely remembered it, stored away in your memory—and tied it behind your neck. The two of you left your room, the night was cool, clouds circled over the property, the chickens were still asleep; and there was your father dressed in his white *clote*, and Tío Meco dressed in a white *clote*, and Tío Abeso dressed in a white *clote*, and you noticed Grandfather Nguema Anseme also was wearing a white *clote*. And you all went into the bush, slowly, Tío Abeso leading the procession, and Grandfather Nguema Anseme bringing up the rear. There was a clear path through the shadows leading to your father's coffee grove; you were all silent, but you could hear a light breeze through the lush foliage covered in dark mist; the moon glowed above, a big moon, round, smiling, and guiding you to the dwelling of the dead, the center of your beginnings and your power. Bare feet crunched lightly over leaves and dry branches; the dew felt moist, sweet and soft, like an intimate prolongation of the silence of your room adorned by the ghosts of a warm and light sleep. Bats could be heard, with their aggressive, anarchic flutter, beguiled, blind in the dark, knocking against the branches, immersed in their own blackness. And above it all, an owl hooted rhythmically from some shadowy limitless spot in the thickness of your mind, and you walked toward it without realizing it, you didn't know or you didn't remember, yes, it was something you had experienced at some other time, these flutterings of ephemeral nature, the cadences of the tribe's eternity, had penetrated your blood—but when, how had it gotten to this path, and why? It could have been in another incarnation, or in dreams, or in the future, or maybe it was something they told me in a story, or maybe I imagined it, or was this path unreal once and for all, twisting, shining, and moving like a serpent toward my father's coffee grove?

But you were not afraid. Because he was there in front of you, cutting a path for you as if he were some kind of precursor. And you followed him, you followed his steps, he was the tireless and benevolent master designated by tradition as the one to show you the way to your lost glory. There he was, firm and steady, with his arms hanging down the length of his broad body, straightening his shoulders in a gesture that flaunted his superiority, those high shoulders accustomed to the weight of a mysterious, magical dignity and the fears of the tribe transmitting his security to you. Then Tío Abeso lifted his round white head toward the moon that was lighting your path and slipping away in the dark sky, less and less visible, and you clearly heard the owl hooting, and you saw it, yes, it was not a dream, and over there the gigantic *ekuk* tree appeared, completely petrified, its four branches the same size as the trunk pointing toward the four directions. And it was surrounded by a dry clearing, parched and dead bushes, a sparkling light coming out of them, perhaps the mysterious, shadowy reflections of a full moon on the withered ground. But what a strange sensation, as if I had always known this place, for they had veiled your memory so that henceforth you could only remember Caesar's *Gallic Wars* and the triumphs of Epaminondas and Saint Augustine's confessions and the *miserere mei Domine*; and the aura of gigantic branches of the gigantic *ekuk* glowed in the darkness, pointing north, south, east, and west, and the croaky mournful hooting of the owl was close by, and you continued slowly on the path toward the dwelling of the dead. And Tío stopped, and you stopped, and the others stopped behind you, and in front of you was the gigantic *ekuk*, and leaning on its roots a bow with no arrow and a bloodied toucan with its three beaks sticking into the ground, and two ants, just two, were crawling into the hollows of its eyes, but they didn't get in all the way; they would retreat and then go back in as if measuring the dark retina, violently brilliant against the light of a warm moon.

Then Tío Abeso circled twice around the gigantic *ekuk*, just twice, and the ants went under the toucan's eyelids, and a very old woman appeared, naked and thin, and she seemed to be blind. An enormous sore made her wrinkled face look hideous, and she asked

Abeso what he was looking for so intently in all the darkness, and he answered that in the dwelling of the dead there is no darkness, and the old woman approached him and asked the same question as if she hadn't heard the answer, and she looked like someone you should have recognized but couldn't. You were confused, the walls had risen, and you would no longer be capable of recognizing the ancestors because your eyesight had been impaired; you couldn't see the old signs, only those of modernity. And the smell of her oozing sore penetrated your nose; I must know how to endure it without fussing or complaining, not to offend her; besides, it would be extremely rude, but really the old lady made you sick, remember? You would have liked it better if you didn't have to see her wrinkles or smell her oozing sores or have to look at her filthy nakedness. My uncle repeated his answer, in the dwelling of the dead there is no darkness, and the old lady then kissed Tío Abeso's hands, and she turned to you and smiled a toothless grin at you, and then she left, waving her arms in the air so as not to bump into imaginary branches or fall over. Tío looked at you, transfigured; his white hair was illuminated, his face emanated a look of dignity, mysterious and magical, his entire body gave out a sense of power, and his breathing was heavy. Grandfather Nguema Anseme, Tío Meco, and your father surrounded you; they too were transfigured, their bodies had acquired a white aura, transparent in the warm moonlight, and your father looked much older to you; and then the old woman came back, and the air was filled with the stench of rotting flesh; she was carrying a huge pot filled with a steaming liquid, and her fragile arms looked as though they were

140

about to break off her emaciated shoulders; and Tío Meco walked into the steam and took hold of a tender palm frond and gave it to Tío Abeso Grandfather Nguema Anseme untied the knot of your white *clote* and you were naked, your body caressed by the gentle morning breeze. And the old woman disappeared, reciting the names of the ancestors and lamenting the loss of glory and the hard times she had to live through.

Tío Abeso spat three times on your face and blessed you; he then dipped the palm frond into the pot, rubbed you with the warm water, and passed the frond to Grandfather Nguema Anseme, who spat three times on your face and blessed you, then dipped the tender frond into the pot, rubbed you with the warm water, and passed the branch to Tío Meco, who spat three times on your face and blessed you, then dipped the tender palm branch into the pot, rubbed you with the warm water, and passed the palm frond back to your father, who spat three times on your face and blessed you, dipped the tender frond into the pot, and rubbed you with the warm water, and then the frond was passed back to Tío Abeso who again spat three times on your face and blessed you, dipped the frond into the pot, rubbed you with the warm water, and passed the branch to Grandfather Nguema Anseme, and it went on like that until the pot was empty. They were transmitting memory to you, intelligence, confidence, honor, respect, strength, patience, understanding, tenderness, and firmness, and all the virtues that would be so necessary in your new life of apprentice wise-man in the long initiation into the white man's school, all those qualities that would be necessary in your new life of apprentice chief so that you could bring back the tribe's glory. And all those qualities penetrated your body and you were anointed with them, an inseparable legacy that has accompanied you since, allowing you to succeed in all the tests devised by the sorcerers of your tribe.

And Tío confirmed you as the heir of the tradition, standing at the foot of the gigantic *ekuk* rising over the tomb of the chiefs of the tribe, and in turn you must transmit this power to a successor chosen by you and accepted by the tribe as long as you are anointed by the mysterious, dangerous, and magical power of the tribe. You must watch over its safety, prosperity, and well-being, and must work tirelessly for its glory, always on the lookout against failure and weakness. And Tío Abeso grabbed the toucan, beheaded it with his hands, and rubbed its blood on your head, and all were silent as the toucan's blood dripped down your face, your neck, your shoulders, your belly, your back, your sex, your legs, and your feet, dropping into the soft mother earth, which then became red. And Tío Abeso offered the toucan to your father, and the gentle morning breeze caressed your cheeks reddened by the blood of the toucan, and the warm smell invaded your lungs, transporting you to a new life, and your emotion deafened you even to Tío Abeso's praise and Grandfather Nguema Anseme's advice. You were happy, remember it, and the breeze began to dry the blood on your body, and the clots stuck to your hair and skin, making them feel extraordinarily heavy, and you learned to endure it all, not like them, and your eyes looked without seeing at the ecstasy-filled eyes of Tío Abeso who was receiving the inspiration of the four branches of the gigantic *ekuk* pointing toward the four directions. And when Grandfather Nguema Anseme told you to pick up the bow and go back to the village, you know the way, you picked up the bow and slowly walked back, full of fervor, still moved by it all, and you barely realized that it was all coming true: the blood was entering your body, leaving your skin soft and smooth. And as the morning became brighter, as the light won over the darkness, as it had always been and would continue to be, as illusion won over tedium, you were thinking of all those wonders, and despite your brief thirteen years, you were convinced that although you would one day cross the ocean and go beyond, you would always have the spirit of the tribe within you, the blood of the tribe, you would always hear the tribe whispering to you.

And of course, we missed the bus because my father was delayed in never-ending farewells, first at Don Santos Casamitjana's trading post, well now you're going to have to work much harder, bring me more coffee and more cocoa, it takes money to have a child in school in Santa Isabel, well what can you do, Don Santos, this is the will of God, and we must accept it and not complain, He sends us children for His glory, and on like that for hours and hours, and my mother crying because I was leaving and listening to Señora M M, and me so happy to be leaving and getting impatient to get on my way, these women always crying about nothing when we're about to miss the bus, and Senora M M so affectionate and so distant, be a good boy, you know your parents sacrifice just for you; yes, Señora; here, these notebooks are for you and remember us from time to time, I'd love to get a few words from you written on this paper; thank you very much Señora. What a nice gesture, my father would say later, this woman is always so thoughtful, she doesn't seem white. And more good-byes with his friends in Territorial Administration, or in the district dispensary, the one they pompously called the Hospital. We must say good bye to Don Placido and Don Prudencio, and Don Serafin, and this one and that one and that guy walking over there; and look, there's Don Esteban fixing his bicycle: you, son, let's see if you behave, our only compensation is to know that you're studying a lot and that you behave so that you'll be an honorable man in this life and deserving of the confidence we have in you, and always be God-fearing. Yes, Papa Placido. Listen, boy, look at your father's sacrifice, working all his life so that you could get to where he never got; yes, Papa Prudencio. Well, my son, you are very fortunate to go and study with the reverend missionary priests, be good and we'll have a priest and when you're ordained remember I held you in my arms; yes Papa Serafin. Here, son, take one hundred pesetas, and be good, your father's making a great sacrifice; thank you Papa Nicolas, thanks very much for the one hundred pesetas, I'll never spend them, I'll just keep them to remember you. Child, since you are so lucky to have a father like the one you have, so sacrificing and such a lover of God, let's see if you deserve the confidence he has in you, you're his firstborn, let's see if you're worthy of your father; yes, Papa Deogracias, such wise advice, I'll remember them all my life and I'll pray for all of you my whole life long, and I'll be as good as I can (but let me leave now because we'll miss the bus, these old folks are driving me crazy, they don't understand we're going to miss the bus). What a well-mannered son you have, man, what good luck to have a firstborn like that, I'm sure he'll grow up to be quite a man, and what a good student he is; true, well, I've never complained, the Lord has given him a good head, I only hope he takes advantage of it for the great glory of the Lord, let's see if your Esteban applies himself too, and the Lord might grant him a vocation; well I'd love that, and if it comes out the way we want I'll see you in Banapa next year if Father Echenagusia allows it. So of course we missed the bus, when we arrived at the African Transport Station Inc, the bus had already started its engine and the baggage handler boy started yelling stop! stop! but the driver didn't hear him; he simply shrugged his shoulders and sat down on a sack of yucca to look at the pretty scenery that extended all the way to Bata. And of course they took my suitcase and everything.

And my father had to rely on Don Santos Casamitjana, the only one we knew who had a private car. Don't say a word, man, I have to go to Bata tomorrow anyway to pick up the goods that just arrived by ship on the Domine Peninsula, it's the same to me if I go this afternoon or tomorrow. I can't tell you how grateful I am, Don Santos, I'll always be grateful. Hey Policarpio, get off your butt, grab the pickup, and take this fine family to Bata, and tomorrow you'd better be back here, no excuses, and stay clear of the ladies and the booze, I know you too well. Don't worry, Mr. Santos; Policarpio the clerk won't touch a drop. And Policarpio the clerk looked down at the ground all humble; how can this guy lie like that, even I heard about the beatings Don Santos Casamitjana gives him every time those pint bottles disappear, and a gentleman like Don Santos couldn't hit anyone if they didn't deserve it; the thing is, Policarpio the clerk is a scoundrel who likes to take a nip or two, and how can Don Santos keep him if so many bottles keep on disappearing? Be quiet, boy, children should stay out of adult conversations. And Policarpio the clerk was a good driver, yes sir; as we rolled down the dusty road toward Bata, he would sing a tune of encouragement to the pickup; get on *piku*, get on *piku*, get on *piku*, and every time he switched gears they would grind so much that it seemed as though the clutch would fall out, and my father wrinkled his brow and asked him if he liked to chew on crabs, and Policarpio the clerk broke out laughing, showing his pure white teeth; he closed his eyes and a little tear came out from laughing so much and everything, and he grabbed on to the steering wheel hard, and my father whispered a little prayer ready to offer his soul to God, and Policarpio the clerk told my father not to worry, that he got along great with this rig, and my father didn't say anything, his eyes fixed on the horizon.

And on the road we passed many huge trucks with markings like Bedford, Saturus, Magirus, Deutz, Mercur, loaded with sacks of coffee or massive tree trunks, and we passed smaller trucks with white passengers and a black chauffeur. Bet you don't know why the whites can make a car but they can't drive them, my friend Ba said to me one afternoon, and I agreed with him, yes, you're right, they don't know how to drive, why is that? Well, it's simple, man, it's their head, it can only think great thoughts, the easy things they leave to the blacks, that's what they're for.

And Policarpio the clerk always tooted his horn when he passed other black chauffeurs, and they tooted back, and when we passed the next car he floored the accelerator and chimed his favorite tune, get on *piku*, get on *piku*, and the pickup kept on going fast into the clouds of dust, and we left the villages behind, and the goats roaming in the middle of the road, and the women carrying baskets on their hunched backs, and the speedometer went toward the limit. And Policarpio the clerk was sweating, not because he was scared but because he was so taken by his own accomplishment, he didn't see the anxiety in my mother's face: why go so fast, my son, we're not in a hurry; don't be afraid, mother, I get along great with this rig, he said, without looking at my mother. And he didn't notice my father's distress either, he was looking at him out of the corner of his eye, and Policarpio the clerk seemed determined to break the speed record, the other drivers were nothing to scoff at; what a guy, I'm the best driver in Continental Spanish Guinea because I'm going 90 klicks an hour on the curves and a hundred on the straight, and my father didn't look at him anymore.

And in spite of it all, we finally made it to Bata. I didn't know I had fallen asleep until my mother pointed at the sea, but its rebellious calm didn't surprise me because I had dreamed about it. It was spectacular because the sun was going down and everything was red, and something told me to look at the sun because a phase of my life was breaking off; I was being pushed away from one world and into another, new and unfamiliar, perhaps red, like a sky about to fall on us, or like the dry earth, its dust settled on everything. From the slight incline that allowed a glimpse of the little houses along the beach, I could see half-naked bodies emerging from behind the grating as they fanned themselves in rocking chairs. And Policarpio the clerk took us to the African Transport Station Inc. to get my suitcase. It's a good thing he went so fast; every cloud has a silver lining, declared my father, and we got there at almost the same time as the bus. The baggage handler boys were still unloading the baskets of yucca and *malanga* and *bipaca* and some other goods I don't know the name of as if the bus were a beast of burden, and the driver of the Bata–Rio Benito Bus was already sitting at the cab with the engine running looking around without seeing the blacks scurrying around and talking loud, the women dressed in multicolored *popos* and the men in short pants, their chests bare, indifferent to the women's chatter. Gentleman-please-for-the-love-of-God-be-so-kind-to-lift-this-basket, one of them pleaded, all out of breath, and the Gentleman just went on patting a friend on the back as if he hadn't seen him for years; they were talking about the fish they had caught in the Mumu River, and the woman made a face as if to say that's life; *aaaaakié*, that's the kind of men we have around here; and she cracked her knuckles and looked away from Gentleman so that she could concentrate on her basket. And the baggage handler boys climbed into the cab of another bus and turned the sign that read Ebebiyin–Bata around so that it now said Bata–Ebebiyin, and in a moment it was on its way to the smelly garage where the buses parked; there were flies swarming around, everyone yelling, banana peels, and rotten man-

148

gos, a bus coming from Evinayong, the driver tooted his horn but no one got out of the way until the bumper brushed against someone's *popo*.

And we went to the house of some kind of relative of my father's in Mbagan; it was a small house typical of that area, the indigenous part of town they called it. The walls were of soft *calabo* and the flat roof was made of tin; it was very cramped, ugly, and hot inside; how can they live their whole lives with this humidity, after all, he's got a government job with the police; it had only one room, and they let my mother and father sleep there while the distant relative went who knows where, and their kids, lots of them, five or six, stayed at the house; I don't think they were allowed to talk to me, at least the girls, because they looked at me shyly from their mat on the floor within an arm's length of mine; they didn't say anything to me the whole night. And in the morning we got up early and left the little house and the neighborhood; see how important it is to have a good head, my son, don't you like sleeping in a bed with clean sheets and not on the floor without anything to cover yourself; yes dad, and this time I really thought my dad was right because I hadn't slept well, the cockroaches crawling on my ears and the mosquitoes getting into my ears; there was no way to get any rest like that, with the girls snoring just an arm's length from me. And I kept thinking about all this when we arrived at the Catholic mission. I think the church in Bata was larger; the mission was just a single wood building painted sloppily, with a slanting roof that looked as if it were about to fall off, and the solitary bell in the solitary belltower in the front of the church was ringing stridently and monotonously when we got to the door. And inside there were uncomfortable benches in crooked lines without back supports and a very plain altar adorned by mildewed paintings with no signature and no beauty, and a single large wooden cross with no Christ at the front of the altar; the whole place had an unusual stamp of severity and primitive piety. It all looked as if it had been put together in haste, constructed in just one night with the miraculous strength of one plump little missionary, neatly dressed, proud, parsimonious, sleepy, and at his side a scabby, crop-headed altar boy.

Everything in the church was an invitation to speak to God in confidence and simplicity, even the tombstone they had placed at the foot of the altar, because, my father told me later—he knew it all—there was going to be a solemn Mass for the eternal repose of the soul of a white man torn apart by a shark on the beach. The shark tore off a buttock, a hand, and then a foot, like that, and this very smart white man ran back and forth along the beach, pursued by a crazy shark, until the shark was washed up on shore. So if this white man was so smart, how come he didn't know there were sharks in those waters, papa? You just be quiet and don't ask silly questions. And when we left the church, still devout and repentant, with the taste of the Host in our mouths, my father showed us the new church they were building: look, this will be the greatest and most beautiful church in all Africa, he told my mother and me, and there were the work crews of blacks toiling to the rhythmic shouts of a brother with his cassock tucked in at the waist, and the brick walls seemed to be climbing pretty high, and yes, I could see the grandness of the new temple erected to the glory of the Virgin of Pilar, and I said to myself that one day I would say Mass on this very altar, yet to be constructed, and that the brother would never shout at me because I was going to be a priest. And from the promontory on which the Catholic mission stood, we could see the beach, its sand white and smooth, sensual and soft, caressed by a light morning breeze, the remains of an old boat washed up on the shore, rusty and black, a boat said to have been sunk by hordes of antichrists, a victim of Satan's army shooting at it with nuns inside and everything, the boat remaining as a symbol of the manly triumph of good over evil, lasting evidence of the ferocious apostates and heretics who wanted to enslave us and strip us from the One True Faith, drowning the Fatherland in a swamp of "isms" when the only acceptable "ism" was Catholicism. Yes, my thoughts were devoted that morning to the commemoration of those brave martyrs who gave their all, every drop of their blood, for the conversion of heathens and the defense of civilization threatened by the enemies of Truth. And the weight of those thoughts would forever be reflected in the photo we took that morning, the first record of my escape from earth, ultimate testimony to my irreversible ascension to the glories of nothingness.

nine

When you all met Father Ortiz that noon at the mission, you didn't know that many, too many, years would pass before you would again walk on that beach, a beach with bubbling waters, in the distance, touched by white foam and bright red clouds of dust. Father Ortiz took your hand when you got out of the mission's Land Rover. The blacks, conquered by the will of the planters, were gathered there with boxes, sacks, packages, wood, themselves determined to initiate a life as conquerors—indecisive, unpracticed, and unwilling, like you, in an unfamiliar island shadowed by mist and covered in black by the vomit of the earth's entrails. Yes, just like you, except that they would break their backs on the plantations and you would genuflect at the altar, initiated into the white man's practice of witchcraft, without knowing that you too would join an invisible army of conquerors attracted to the island's riches. The planter had told them they would find good pay for their work, fine women, taverns just for blacks, a short distance from Santa Isabel but you'll be able to do what you want there, not like on the mainland, where you have to hide your drink; you'll have good strong brandy; here, take three hundred pesetas for your girlfriend's dowry and come with me to Fernando Poo for a couple of years, only four work seasons, and when you go back you'll be top man in town, the envy of your townspeople. And the black man rolled his eyes, and he took the three hundred pesetas that to him meant fine women and good strong brandy; happiness was promised, so now he dozed off among the boxes, the sacks, and packages. And off they all went, determined to cross the hundred and twenty-five miles even if they had to swim so that they could be the new bosses in town; they would stay on the mysterious island forever, slaves of modernity, or they would return with cheap jewelry for the women. And you would return many years later, carrying the wisdom and power of the whites, determined to be the new boss in town. Your mother was crying, but you didn't see her because you were busy thinking about your victorious return, dressed in a black cassock and blue sash that would give you the perpetual immunity necessary for the salvation of the tribe. Your father was crying, but you didn't see him, you saw yourself as a replica of Father Ortiz imbued with his mysterious, magical power, which, together with the mysterious, magical dignity of the ancestors, had been granted to you; it would give you the strength and valor necessary to consolidate the triumph. And this is why, at the last farewell, you told them, I'll be back; you said this with enthusiasm, with affection, with love, but also with a certain bitterness.

They were carrying bundles, oil lamps, a mattress, a sack of *malanga*, and the one at your side wearing a grotesque helmet from some mysterious war the whites had fought among themselves, who knows when. But you, recalling it many years later when you read about the heroic feats of that war, identified it as a German helmet. But of course the man wearing it didn't know; he just played his *oyeng* guitar as he walked across the beach toward the canoe, and the music was sad and lonely echoing from the waters, as if he were playing a farewell tune from the tribe. A tall, muscular black man took Father Ortiz in his arms and carried him like a small child, bringing him over the water, and you looked at his pith helmet dancing on his round crown: What if the black man trips and the priest falls into the water? What a joke! But they got to the boat safely, the black man didn't trip, and the priest didn't fall into the water; he was placed in the center of the boat with all the care in the world, not a drop spattered on his clean cassock, recently ironed by the nuns in the nearby school. The black man then walked toward you and grabbed your suitcase and Father Ortiz's as well, along with the black handbag, and brought them to the boat. And then he came over to you; your mother tried to hug you for the last time, but you preferred the arms of the black man interrupting your mother's embrace, seized by the emotions of a future about to begin; my poor mother, she was afraid of my missing the boat, and she didn't know that so many long years would go by; if she had, she wouldn't have hastened her embrace. They were crying in silence, watching you take your leave like a white dignitary in the arms of the strong black man, but you were looking straight ahead, without tears, eyes dry, absorbed in the image of the ship anchored in the middle of the ocean; these whites sure know a lot, look at that heavy metal boat floating in the water when a little stone goes right to the bottom; blacks aren't even capable of making a needle while the whites make ships and everything, and I'm going to gain wisdom, because the priest is the wisest of the whites. The black man set you down in the boat next to Father Ortiz, and you saw yourself in his clear eyes; you were calm and confident as always when you were with him, just as you were when you went to the chapel in the part of the forest that was cleared out, and you were behind him on the motorbike. The bush was fading behind us, the palm trees were getting smaller, and the ship was getting larger; my it's big, heavens! those whites sure know a lot, and Father Ortiz knows more than any of them, that's why he's a priest, and I'll be as wise as him, that's why I'm going to the seminary.

And you took your last look back, remember? as if to confirm to yourself that you had left your dear motherland behind for good, or as a desire to preserve the face of your mother, my poor mother, but they had already disappeared from your view and your life. They had gone with the breeze, devoured by the coconut trees or sheltered by the palm trees on the beach, and you were now alone with Father Ortiz in the space between the past and future, and the present was a black man rowing in silence toward the ship, the water as clear as a mirror, majestic and deep, and you dipped your hand into the water to feel the Atlantic for the first time; they told me it was salty, let's see

155

if it's true, and the oarsman said something to you that you didn't understand, remember? It was the first time you heard a black man speak in a language other than Fang; he must be Combe or Bujeba, who knows, and you understood the priest but not the Combe or Bujeba; don't put your hand in the water, it's dangerous; civilization has ordered it so, to be confined in the boat, understanding the priest and not the Combe or Bujeba. And when you got to the steps leading into the ship and Father Ortiz gave the Combe or Bujeba a picture of the Sacred Heart of Mary taken from the book of prayers he always kept in the pocket of his cassock, you started climbing up, in front of the priest, carrying your suitcase and his black handbag with a little metal cross on one of its sides, and in front of you was the radiant backside of a beautiful black woman, but you didn't see her, inhibited as you were by contemplating the white man's accomplishments: the ship was huge, painted a brilliant white, and everywhere you could see its printed name, Domine-Valencia, and that name was a premonition, because you were on your way to the Lord, in the arms of the Lord. Next to you, white men were shouting at the black recruits, eh! hop! quicker! lively now!—curses and insults that tapered off when they sensed the presence of Father Ortiz; they were caught off guard and apologized to the priest, sorry Father, there's just no way to deal with them, but you didn't hear this, just like the rest of the blacks, who didn't understand the white man's language, for you yourself didn't want to hear about the misery of this world, absorbed as you were in thoughts of the future, a future you were entering in the midst of the sweet-smelling breeze and the strong smell of the

156

ship, its oils, and a thousand unfamiliar odors.

A burly sailor, with stern gestures and arms extended, showed the black women their seats in front of you, and he showed you yours, on the top next to some cows that would serve as meals for the return trip to the Peninsula. But the priest took you by the hand, making sure you were not taken for any little black boy. Sorry Father, the sailor excused himself, I didn't know he was with you, and another sailor showed you the way down the hidden corridors of that dazzling city afloat. You both went down some stairs and found yourselves in perfectly arranged cabin chambers with the bed made and a cross on the wall, all in harmony with the movement of the calm waters of the Atlantic. When you both went up again to the upper deck, you saw the blacks all piled together on rickety wood smoothed by the water washing against it and still damp from the last swabbing of the deck; the blacks tried to arrange themselves any way they could amidst the cargo. You went over to the railing and looked at the sea, it was huge, murky and thick, and the moon was now shining through the black clouds even though the sun had yet to disappear into the red horizon, and you knew it was going to rain.

And more blacks boarded, all huddling together: old folks, young people, infants. And the black man with the helmet and guitar sat down protected from the rain and began strumming; it was a distant rhythm, strange and warm, and stayed with you all afternoon, through the long, rainy night; it was with you in your cabin as the ship cut through the gulf. Many years later you would still sway to the pulse of that rocking motion, cradled by the waves and the warm music of the *oyeng* guitar.

Translator's Postscript

"You understood the priest but not the Combe or Bujeba." So says the narrator-protagonist in one of the final scenes of this unique African novel. It is something of a cathartic sentence; the speaker seems to have come to an understanding of himself—his history and identity. After the arduous work of (re)collecting his entire life in Equatorial Guinea (the only Spanish-speaking country in sub-Saharan Africa), that long struggle both to remember and to retain his "Africanness," a struggle that comprises the entire novel, the reader, along with the protagonist, begins to fathom the complexity of identity itself: personal, ethnic, national, religious, existential. The protagonist's understanding of Father Ortiz, his would-be mentor and colonial father-figure, goes well beyond an understanding of the words he speaks. Throughout the novel we surmise that the protagonist clearly understands the intricacies and contradictions of Father Ortiz better than the priest does himself. But at the same time, as the protagonist begins his journey out of Africa and into the world of those who colonized it, he understands the irony that he is unable to comprehend the words of his own people since they are not of his tribe, a reality that will destabilize his self and his being for the rest of his life. It is perhaps a lesson for all of us: when we think we have come to an understanding of who we are, a fact, or an incident, or a new phase of our life arises annoyingly to question that understanding.

Such self-questioning is felt throughout this novel, not only on the level of an individual psyche, but in the broader public domain as well. Indeed, the protagonist's inner search for authenticity is a collective one. *Shadows of Your Black Memory* contains all the social expansiveness of a bildungsroman, the story of a boy growing into manhood during the last years of Spain's colonial rule in Equatorial Guinea. It is also a book of memories: in the present of the narrative the boy is grown and living in Spain. The memories are themselves an exploration of how he arrived at the land that has become the object of all the tensions, quandaries, disquiet, and understated anger that fuel his introspection. And clearly Spain has much to do with the disquiet. Two worlds—Africa and Europe—are constantly juxtaposed, not unlike the framework of Chinua Achebe's famous *Things Fall Apart,* in which "things" refer to an existence before the arrival of the Europeans. And as "things fall apart" at the hands of colonial power, we witness the collapse of a way of life, indeed the fall of "civilization." In *Shadows* that collapse develops in the form of a subtle coercion of a boy into the priesthood and away from his tradition in deference not only to the colonizers but to his father and mother, devout Catholics who have been well taught about the needed advancement (economic, moral, technological) of their native land—Frantz Fanon would say they have been taught to wear white masks. Yet throughout the novel we find hints of resistance, which is, after all, the motive for the memories. Tío Abeso, a revered uncle and something of a counter-mentor to the boy, does not speak Spanish; he is a polygamist; he believes in the power of the tribe's ancestors rather than in Christ or any of the colonizers' deities; and he insists on providing his precocious nephew with the rituals that constitute the steps to manhood, including circumcision.

But *Shadows* as a forum for competing cosmologies has a context as well, absolutely crucial for the novel's understanding. This Spanish-African narrative takes place in a part of Africa in dire need of attention from those comfortably living in the global "North," not only for its rich culture but for its all too typical political problems. Equatorial Guinea is both unique and typical among postcolonial African nations—unique for its predominantly Spanish-speaking populace, and emblematic of the economic and political hardships that have plagued the majority of African nations after independence. The former Spanish colony constitutes the main island of Bioko (or Fernando Poo in colonial times), as well as Annabon, Corisco, and the two islands of Elobey, all in the Gulf of Guinea. There is also a continental area known as Río Muni (Ndongo's birthplace) that borders on Gabon and Cameroon. Although the main ethnic groups (Bubi, Ndowe, Fang, Annabonese, and the Fernandinos) are distinguished by their own customs and languages, Spanish remains the lingua franca and Spanish colonialism the historical mainstay of the entire nation. Ndongo's ethnicity is Fang; yet like many Equatorial Guineans he is familiar with the other cultures of his nation. The strangeness of this novel, the difficulty of situating it within a more recognizable tradition of literature in Spanish is due in part to this very multiplicity of languages and cultures. The Fernandinos, for example, are Creole descendents of slaves mainly from Nigeria and Sierra Leone and speak a form "pichín," or pidgin English, due to the influence of protestant missionaries as well as Nigerian contract laborers brought in to work on the plantations. As one notes from the text of the novel and the accompanying glossary, English terms such as "country tea" morphed in pichín into *contrití*. *Clote* is another example, derived from "clothes" or "cloth." Yet for all the native African languages and dialects, the author of *Shadows* has said that the precarious unity of Equatorial Guinea rests more than anything on the Spanish language, perhaps the most telling indicator of the nation's (and the author's) bicultural condition—African and Spanish.

In many ways Ndongo falls into the patterns of African intellectuals and creative writers. Born in Niefang (1950), near Bata, the main city of Río Muni, and sent by his family in 1965 to study in Valencia and finish his secondary education, he perfected not only the language of the country that colonized him but its ways—its foibles, contradictions, strengths, and weaknesses. News of the 1968 independence was bitter-sweet; within months, the country had been taken over by a brutal dictator, Francisco Macías. Ndongo describes this period with glaring detail in his subsequent novel, *Los poderes de la tempestad* (Powers of the Tempest). Atrocities committed by Macías were known as the *años de silencio* (years of silence) when news of the oppression—much by word of mouth—trickled into Spain. The Franco government had devised the policy of *materia reservada*, classifying all information concerning Equatorial Guinea in the immediate years following independence. Thus Ndongo made the first of many decisions typical of exile writers all over the world: he would remain out of his country as long as the dictator was in power. In 1969 he began his studies at the University of Barcelona (Central) with a concentration in African history. From 1972 well into the mid-seventies his activities as a journalist brought him into the fray of the momentous events in Spanish history known as *la transición* (the transition from dictatorship to democracy). He wrote for several Spanish news journals, predominantly *Indice* and *Mundo Negro*, the latter of which remains an outlet for his writing today. In 1977 he turned some of his journalistic work on Equatorial Guinea into a book, *Historia y tragedia de Guinea Ecuatorial* (History and Tragedy of Ecuatorial Guinea), which was at that time, thanks to *materia reservada*, the only published information on the carnage of the Macías regime.

In the seventies and eighties Ndongo would spend most his effort writing about Africa for the Spanish press: *Indice, Mundo Negro, Diario 16, Historia 16, ABC,* and the wire service EFE. During this time he became the director of a residence hall close to the University of Madrid (Complutense), Nuestra Señora de Africa, that made an attempt to accommodate Africans studying in Spain by organizing cultural activities and assisting African students in their dealings with Spanish immigration bureaucracy. Working with these African students was more than an occupation for Ndongo; it reflects his leadership role as an advocate of African issues and rights in Spain, a role that he will later assume as the director of the Hispano-Guinean Cultural Center in Malabo. As a person with firsthand experience with migration from Africa to Europe, he made that experience a collective one. Given the low numbers of Africans living in Spain at that time, the uniqueness of his condition as a Guinean dissident living in Spain made the focus on that activity all the more intense. Indeed, being black in the Spain of the 1970s was something of a "beginning intention" for his writing, as Edward Said calls it in *Beginnings*, a first thought that informs both his individual psyche and his status as a member of a group.

In 1979 there was a coup plotted by Macías's nephew, Teodoro Obiang, the present leader of the country. But little changed; Obiang did away with the previous dictator but not with the system of oppression. With Obiang in power and his false promises of opening the society, Ndongo made a quixotic (perhaps even contradictory) decision to return to his native land definitively—or so he thought—in 1985 as the director of the Hispano-Guinean Cultural Center in Malabo (Bioko). That period of his life was filled with turmoil due to his reporting of incidents similar to those perpetrated by the previous dictator. When in 1992 he left the cultural center to become a full-time journalist covering African affairs for EFE, a position that made his objections even more visible and hard-hitting for the Obiang regime, his situation in the country became more precarious than it had ever been. So much so, that he fled from Malabo to Libreville, Gabon, where he spent another year with EFE before returning to Spain definitively in 1994.

However, for all of Ndongo's journalistic, political, and administrative activity, he has said that his prime desire is to write fiction, and his fiction is informed by his émigré status. *Los poderes de la tempestad* (1997) is the continuation of *Shadows*: the protagonist is a grown man, a lawyer married to a white woman who comes back to his country from Spain to test the waters of independence only to find horrific repression—mass killings, fear, squalor, ironically an atmosphere worse than that of the colony. Most recently Ndongo has tackled the issue of immigration with a novel titled *El metro,* in which the central character is a Cameroonian who decides to leave his family and his culture in search of a new and more prosperous way of life in Europe. It is the story of thousands of Africans living in Spain today, as immigration has become one of the Iberian Peninsula's most controversial topics, a topic familiar to virtually all societies of the global "North."

Undeniably, Ndongo's fiction manifests the familiar tensions between the realities of African life and their fictional representation, ambivalences felt by many exile writers as well as migrants regarding the new home. Although Spain is the home of necessity, it shapes the author as much as Africa does. A man of political convictions, Ndongo was influenced by the most important social developments in Spain in the second half of the twentieth century: the Franco dictatorship and its aftermath, the alienation and disenchantment of a post-civil-war left that was tired of dictatorship and determined to recover a socialist history and social "progress" broken by the war. Yet he was also deeply affected by broader global movements such as the struggles for independence of former African colonies, in his case the most important one being his native Equatorial Guinea. The fact that he begins to write fiction in the wake of both *negritude* and the immediate aftermath of Franco allows him a certain distance from those two cultural-political phenomena. It also allows him a way of predicting the pitfalls of the newly achieved self-determinations, both Spain's and Equatorial Guinea's.

Indeed, Ndongo was and remains a resident of Spain, an African stranger in a land familiar to him, and as such he is intricately connected to the patterns of Spanish intellectuals of his time (many of whom were his friends), while at the same time remaining unique, other. Not that his fellow writers and friends—Alfonso Grosso, Juan Madrid, Claudio Rodríguez, Antonio Ferres, along with a host of socialist politicians such as Fernando Morán, Raul Modoro, Enrique Múgica—were not interested in the writing of Aimé Césaire, Léopold Senghor, or Frantz Fanon. Ndongo was exceptional in that circle in the seventies because he was strange: a colonial subject of flesh and bone—we needn't forget skin. His writing manifests that subjectivity on virtually every page. Writing from the subject position of a black man is uncommon (if not completely absent) in the annals of Spanish literature. Ndongo's texts manifest a postcolonial otherness: he is in conflict with the political and social surroundings emanating from Francoisim, and he is black. In light of these "othering" forces, Frantz Fanon's famous work, *Black Skin, White Masks*, has had a lasting affect on Ndongo.

Clearly, along with the vicissitudes of identity and race construction, Ndongo's lasting concern in his fiction has been colonialism and its "dark idea"—as Joseph Conrad called it in *Heart of Darkness*. Yet perhaps due to the very power of this "idea" as it continued to manifest itself in Equatorial Guinea in its post-independence, Ndongo has established himself as an exceptional writer in the "land of Cervantes." With *Shadows* followed by *Powers*, along with several short stories, poetry, and his most recent novel, *El metro*, one could say that Spanish Africa has produced a postcolonial writer of the same ilk and with the same preoccupations as those of Chinua Achebe and Wole Soyinka. And with the "darkening" of the Spanish population due to rapid immigration from the global "South" and growing racial awareness on the part of residents of the European country closest to Africa, Ndongo is an African voice in a country deeply ambivalent about its own African past. Indeed, he is a person whose writing will entice readers to explore that universal relationship between self and other.

Note on Translation

Rendering Donato Ndongo's Spanish prose into English presents a variety of problems, interesting ones. The vast majority of both English and Spanish readers are unaware of the customs, languages, and everyday life in Equatorial Guinea, and even more so when that life takes place during the colonial period as does Ndongo's novel. Words such as *contrití*, *clote*, or *pikú* (pick-up truck) are as baffling to Spanish as to English-speaking readers. Thus I have decided to keep the Guinean word used in the Spanish original and provide a glossary of terms with specific cultural meanings. The uniqueness of *Shadows* within the canon of twentieth-century literature written in Spanish should be reflected in the translation.

Yet even more problematic for a translator of Ndongo's writing is his intricate style: sentences that go on for over half a page and paragraphs that seem endless. This intricacy arises from the fact that the protagonist's story is a recollection. Ndongo's use of both the first and second person attests to the intricacies of memory, as he creates an interior dialogue within the protagonist's psyche, a conversation between his present self living in Spain and his past self as a lad in the environs of colonial Bata. This dialogue manifests the protagonist's cultural identity with all its contradictions and uncertainties. Thus the task for the translator is to remain faithful to the tone of inner interrogation while at the same time rendering accessible the many episodes of the protagonist's life—his relationship with his mother and father and, of course, Tío Abeso; his first sexual encounter; his observation and description of the exuberant natural world that surrounds and nurtures him. This has involved a difficult balance between a certain hermeticism, a deliberate lack of clarity, arising from the slipperiness of memory on the one hand and a discernable plot on the other, a story with a beginning, a middle, and an end. At times I have tried to solve this problem by breaking the sentences up in particularly labyrinthine stylistic moments or inserting a semicolon every now and then. I hope this has led to a marriage between the stream-of-consciousness flow of the narrative and the understandability of specific happenings in the plot.

Having the author only a phone call away, always willing to help me understand the details of a particular situation, a word, or an element of the tropical natural environment, has been invaluable. *Chapeau* to those translators who produce beautifully rendered texts without such help. I can only hope that I have been faithful to the novelist's prose. I want to express my deepest gratitude to Donato Ndongo for having written such an engaging and troubling novel. I also want to thank the following people who read the translated manuscript in its entirety and offered valuable suggestions, virtually all of which have improved the translation: Professor Trudy Lewis of the University of Missouri—Columbia, Professor Susan Martin-Márques of Rutgers University; and from Swan Isle, David Rade, and Margaret Mahan.

Glossary

aaaaakié! (akié!). Fang: interjection to express astonishment or disgust.

akoma. First wife in a polygamous marriage.

atanga. Cylindrical, hard, purple fruit with green pulp and a large pit; usually boiled.

bambucha. Name used by Spaniards for a staple dish in the Fang diet made with yucca leaves, pulp of dates, palm oil, hot peppers, *malanga*, and other greens.

bea. Red paint derived from plants; used in war and also in religious ceremonies, along with *ekuuan*.

bipaca. Fang: salted fish.

Bujeba. Ethnic group related to the Combe, residing in the coastal area.

calabo. Light wood, easy to carve; used in construction of walls for dwellings.

clote. "Pichín" or Pidgin English: fabric, usually multicolored, worn by men; comes from the English word "cloth."

Combe. Ethnic group related to the Bujeba, residing in the coastal area; same as Ndowé, one of several "playero" groups.

contrití. "Pichín": tea made from leaves of a plant with the same name; comes from the English words "country tea."

Djoba, Nguema y Bokesa. Title of a textbook used in the colonial educational curriculum; it represents the three main ethnic groups of Equatorial Guinea: Djoba ("playeros"), Nguema (Fang), and Bokesa (Bubi).

egombegombe. Word used by Spaniards, designating a tree with a straight trunk and leaves in the form of an umbrella; a good source of shade; its fruit is well liked by children.

ekuk. Tree whose trunk, leaves, and latex are used as a traditional medicine to treat various diseases such as diarrhea, malaria, and worms.

ekuuan. White clay found on the banks of rivers and brooks, used as an ornamental body paint for various rituals; not to be confused with "ekuan" meaning banana.

emancipado. Spanish for "emancipated." An emancipated Guinean was an indigenous person who was officially recognized as having all the rights of a Spaniard.

malanga. Spanish: arum; tuber similar to but tastier than yucca; its leaves are also used as a condiment.

melongo. Fang: an aquatic plant that grows in marshes; its stem is flexible yet hard and is used as a stick to discipline children; it may also be used to tie objects together.

oyeng. The correct term in Fang is nvet oyeng; a stringed musical instrument that accompanies storytellers in oral literature; the author used "oyeng" to make the concept accessible to Spanish speakers.

popo. Fang: in Spanish pronounced "popó"; multicolored fabric used to make female garments.

sixas. Older unmarried women (usually in their forties) who generally lived alongside the female missionaries or under the supervision of a catechist; in colonial times they were given classes dealing with hygiene, domestic work, and religion.

tío, tía. Spanish for "uncle," "aunt."

tumba. Percussion instrument made from a hollowed tree; used as an instrument of communication among various tribes and villages; also used as a call to initiate a religious rite, as a chapel bell.

wambas. Moccasins, sandals.

Names of Places

Bata: Largest city in Rio Muni, on the Atlantic coast; population around 50,000.

Ebebeyin: Town in the northeastern corner of Rio Muni, on the border of Cameroon and Gabon.

Fernando Poo: Colonial name given to the island of Bioko, Equatorial Guinea.

Santa Isabel: Colonial name given to Malabo, capital of Eqatorial Guinea, on the island of Bioko.

For Further Reading

Fanon, Frantz. *Black Skin, White Masks*. Translated by Charles Lam Markmann. New York: Grove, 1967.

Fra-Molinero, Baltasar. "La educación sentimental de un exiliado africano: *Las tinieblas de tu memoria negra*, de Dontato Ndongo-Bidyogo. *Afro-Hispanic Review* 19, no. (2000): 49–57.

Klitgaard, Robert E. *Tropical Gangsters: One Man's Experience with Development and Decadence in Deepest Africa*. New York: Basic Books, 1990.

Kucich, John. *Fictions of Empire: Complete Texts, with Introduction, Historical Contexts, Critical Essays*. New Riverside Editions. New York: Houghton Mifflin, 2003.

Liniger-Goumaz, Max. *De la Guinée Ecuatorial: Eléments pour le dossier de l'afrofascisme*. Geneva: Les Editions de Temps, 1983.

———. *Small Is Not Always Beautiful: The Story of Equatorial Guinea*. Translated by John Wood. Totowa, NJ: Barnes and Noble: 1989.

Maass, Peter. "A Touch of Crude." *Mother Jones,* January–February 2005, *www.motherjones.com*

Mengue, Clarence. "Lectura del espacio en *Los poderes de la tempes-tad* de Donato Ndongo." *Arizona Journal of Hispanic Cultural Studies* 8 (2004): 185–95.

Ndongo-Bidyogo, Donato. "El metro" (chap. 13 of the 2007 novel; see next entry). *Granta en Español: La última frontera* 3 (Fall–Winter 2005): 259–72.

Ndongo-Bidyogo, Donato. *El metro*. Barcelona: Ediciones del Cobre, 2007.

———. "El sueño." In Ndongo-Bidyogo and Ngom, *Literatura de Guinean Ecuatorial (Antología)* (see below), 204–7.

———. *Historia y tragedia de Guinea Ecuatorial*. Madrid: Cambio 16, 1977.

———. *Las tinieblas de tu memoria negra*. Madrid: Fundamentos, 1987; Barcelona: Ediciones del Bronce, 2000.

———. "Los herederos del Señor Kurtz." In *El planeta Kurtz: Cien años de 'El corazón de las tinieblas' de Joseph Conrad*, edited by José Luis Marzo y Marc Roig, 123–40. Barcelona: Mondadori, 2002.

———. *Los poderes de la tempestad*. Madrid: Morandi, 1997.

Ndongo-Bidyogo, Donato, Mariano Castro, and José Urbano Mar-tínez. *España en Guinea: Construcción del desencuentro: 1778-1968*. Madrid: Sequitur, 1998.

Ndongo-Bidyogo, Donato, and Mbaré Ngom, eds. *Literatura de Gui-*

nean Ecuatorial (Antología). Madrid: Casa de Africa, Sial, 2000.

Nerín, Gustau. *Guinea Ecuatorial: historia en blanco y negro* Barcelona: Peninsula1998.

N'gom, M'baré, ed. "Guinea Ecuatorial: textos y contextos culturales e históricos." Special issue, *Afro-Hispanic Review* 19, no. 1 (2000).

————. "La autobiografía como plataforma de denuncia en *Los Poderes de la tempestad.*" Special issue, *Afro-Hispanic Review* 19, no. 1 (2000): 66–71.

Nsue Otong, Carlos. "Estudios de los personajes en *Las tinieblas de tu memoria negra* de Donato Ndongo-Bidyogo." *Afro-Hispanic Review* 19.1 (2000): 58–65.

Price, Nicole. "'Materia Reservada' No More: The Postcolonial in the Equato-Guinean Narrative." Diss., University of Missouri–Columbia, 2005.

Senghor, Leopold. *Chants d'ombre, suivi de Hosties noires: Poèmes.* Paris: Seuil: 1945.

Silverstein, Ken. "U.S. Oil Politics in the 'Kuwait of Africa.'" *The Nation,* April 22, 2002, 11–20.

Ugarte, Michael. "An Introduction to Postcolonial Exile: The Narrative of Donato Ndongo." *Arizona Journal of Hispanic Cultural Studies* 8 (2004): 177–84.

————. "Interview With Donato Ndongo." *Arizona Journal of Hispanic Cultural Studies* 8 (2004): 217–34.

———. "Spain's 'Heart of Darkness': Equatorial Guinea in the Narrative of Donato Ndongo." Special issue titled "African Spain," edited by Michael Ugarte and Teresa Vilarós, *Journal of Spanish Cultural Studies* 7, no. 3 (2006): 271–87.

Ugarte, Michael, and M'baré N'gom. *Equatorial Guinea in Spanish Letters*. Special section of *Arizona Journal of Hispanic Cultural Studies* 8 (2004): 105–245.

See also ASODEGUE (Asociación de Solidaridad con Guinea Ecuatorial): www.asodegue.org as well as the Wikipedia entry on Equatorial Guinea, which provides a brief explanation of that country's culture and history.

Swan Isle Press is a not-for-profit publisher
of poetry, fiction, and nonfiction.

For information on books of related interest or
for a catalog of new publications contact:

www.swanislepress.com

Shadows of Your Black Memory
Designed by Edward Hughes
Typeset in New Aster
Printed on 55# Glatfelter Natural